THE SIGN AT SIX

Helen

The Sign at Six

BY STEWART EDWARD WHITE

Author of "The Blazed Trail," etc.

With Four Illustrations
By M. LEONE BRACKER

WILDSIDE PRESS

CONTENTS

THE SIGN AT SIX

CHAPTER I

THE OWNER OF NEW YORK

PERCY DARROW, a young man of scientific training, indolent manners, effeminate appearance, hidden energy, and absolute courage, lounged through the doors of the Atlas Building. Since his rescue from the volcanic island that had witnessed the piratical murder of his old employer, Doctor Schermerhorn, the spectacular dissolution of the murderers, and his own imprisonment in a cave beneath the very roar of an eruption, he had been nursing his shattered nerves back to their normal strength. Now he felt that at last he was able to go to work again. Therefore, he was about

I

The Sign at Six

to approach a man of influence among practical scientists, from whom he hoped further occupation.

As the express elevator shot upward, he passed a long slender hand across his eyes. The rapid motion confused him still. The car stopped, and the metallic gates clanged open. Darrow obediently stepped forth. Only when the elevator had disappeared did his upward glance bring to him the knowledge that he had disembarked one floor too soon.

Darrow's eye fell on a lettered sign outside the nearest door. He smiled a slow red-lipped smile beneath his small silky mustache, drooped his black eyelashes in a flicker of reminiscence, hesitated a moment, then stepped languidly forward and opened the door. The sign indicated the headquarters of the very modest commissionership behind which McCarthy chose to work. McCarthy, quite simply, at that time owned New York.

The Sign at Six

As Darrow entered, McCarthy hung up the telephone receiver with a smash, and sat glaring at the instrument. After a moment he turned his small bright eyes toward the newcomer.

"Hello, Perc," he growled. "Didn't see you. Say, I'm so mad my skin cracks. Just now some measly little shrimp called me up from a public booth. What ye suppose he wanted, now? Oh, nothin'! Just told me in so many words for me to pack up my little trunk and sail for Europe and never come back! That's all! He give me until Sunday, too." McCarthy barked out a short laugh, and reached for the cigar box, which he held out to Darrow.

Percy shook his head. "What's the occasion?" he asked.

"Oh, I don't know. Just bughouse, I guess."

"So he wants you to go to Europe?"

"Wants me? Orders me! Says I got to." McCarthy laughed. "Lovely thought!"

3

The Sign at Six

He puffed out a cloud of smoke.

"Says if I don't obey orders he'll send me a 'sign' to convince me!" went on the boss. "He's got a mean voice. He ought to have a tag hung on him and get carried to the morgue. He give me the shivers, like a dead man. I never hear such a unholy thing outside a grave-yard at midnight!"

Percy Darrow was surveying him with lei-surely amusement, a slight smile playing over his narrow dark face.

"Talking to get back your nerve," he sur-mised cheerfully to the usually taciturn boss. "I'd like to know what it was got you going so; it isn't much your style."

"Well, you got yours with you," growled McCarthy, shifting for the first time from his solid attitude of the bulldog at bay.

"His 'sign' he promised is apt to be a bomb," observed Darrow.

"He's nutty, all right," McCarthy agreed,

4

The Sign at Six

"but when he said that, he was doing the tall religious. He's got a bug that way."

"Your affair," said Darrow. "Just the same, I'd have an outer office."

"Outer office—rot!" said the boss. "An outer office just gets cluttered up with people waiting. Here they've got to say it right out in meeting—if I want 'em to. What's the good word, Perc? What can I do for you?"

Darrow smiled. "You know very well, my fat friend, that the only reason you like me at all is that I'm the one and only man who comes into this office who doesn't want one single thing of you."

"I suppose that's it," agreed McCarthy. The telephone rang. He snatched down the receiver, listened a moment, and thrust forward his heavy jowl. "Not on your life!" he growled in answer to some question. While he was still occupied with the receiver, Percy Darrow nodded and sauntered out.

CHAPTER II

DARROW walked up the one flight of steps to the story above. He found his acquaintance in, and at once broached the subject of his errand. Doctor Knox promised the matter his attention. The two men then embarked on a long discussion of Professor Schermerhorn's discovery of super-radium, and the strange series of events that had encompassed his death. Into the midst of the discussion burst McCarthy, his face red with suppressed anger.

"Can I use your phone?" he growled. "Oh, yes," said he, as he caught sight of the instrument. Without awaiting the requested per-

6

The Sign at Six

mission, he jerked the receiver from its hook and placed it to his ear.

"Deader than a smelt!" he burst out. "This is a nice way to run a public business! Thanks," he nodded to Doctor Knox, and stormed out.

Darrow rose languidly.

"I'll see you again," he told Knox. "At present I'm going to follow the human cyclone. It takes more than mere telephones to wake McCarthy up like that."

He found the boss in the hall, his finger against the "down" button.

"That's three cars has passed me," he snarled, trying to peer through the ground glass that, in the Atlas Building, surrounded the shaft. "I'll tan somebody's hide. Down!" he bellowed at a shadow on the glass.

"Have a cigarette," proffered Percy Darrow. "Calm down. To the scientific eye you're out of condition for such emotions. You thick-necks are subject to apoplexy."

7

The Sign at Six

"Oh, shut up!" growled McCarthy. "There isn't a phone in order in this building two floors either way. I've tried 'em—and there hasn't been for twenty minutes. And I can't get a messenger to answer a call; and that ring-tailed, star-spangled ornament of a janitor won't answer his private bell. I'll get him bounced so high the blackbirds will build nests in his ear before he comes down again."

After trying vainly to stop a car on its way up or down, McCarthy stumped down a flight of stairs, followed more leisurely by the calmly unhurried Darrow. Here the same performance was repeated. A half dozen men by now had joined them. So they progressed from story to story until an elevator boy, attracted by their frantic shouts, stopped to see what was the matter. Immediately the door was slid back on its runners, McCarthy seized the astonished operator by the collar.

"Come out of that, you scum of the earth!"

8

McCarthy stumped down a flight of stairs

The Sign at Six

he roared. "Come out of that and tell me why you don't stop for your signals!"

"I ain't seen no signals!" gasped the elevator boy.

Some one punched the button, but the little, round, annunciator disk in the car failed to illuminate.

"I wonder if there's anything in order in this miserable hole!" snarled McCarthy.

"The lights is gone out," volunteered the boy; and indeed for the first time the men now crowding into the car noticed that the incandescents were dead.

While McCarthy stormed out to spread abroad impartial threats against two public utility concerns for interfering with his business, Percy Darrow, his curiosity aroused, interviewed the janitor. Under that functionary's guidance he examined the points of entrance for the different wires used for lighting and communication; looked over the private-

9

The Sign at Six

bell installations, and ascended again to the corridor, abstractedly dusting his fingers. There he found a group of the building's tenants, among whom he distinguished Doctor Knox.

"Same complaint, I suppose—no phones, no lights, no bells," he remarked.

"Seems to be," replied Knox. "General condition. Acts as though the main arteries had been cut outside."

"Inside bells? House phones?" suggested Darrow.

The repair men came in double-quick time and great confidence. They went to work in an assured manner, which soon slackened to a slower bewilderment. Some one disappeared, to return with a box of new batteries. The head repair man connected a group of these with a small bell in the executive office. The instrument, however, failed to respond.

"Try your ammeter," suggested Darrow, who had followed.

The Sign at Six

The delicate needle of the instrument did not quiver.

"Batteries dead!" said the repair man. "Jim, what the hotel-bill do you mean by getting dead batteries? Go back and bring a new lot, and *test* 'em."

In due time Jim returned.

"These test to fifteen," said he. "Go to it!"

"Test—nothing!" roared the repair man after a moment. "These are dead, too."

Percy Darrow left the ensuing argument to its own warmth. It was growing late. In the corridor a few hastily-brought lamps cast a dim light. Percy collided against Doctor Knox entering the building.

"Not fixed yet?" asked the latter in evident disappointment. "What's the matter?"

"I don't know," said Darrow slowly; "it puzzles me. It's more than an ordinary break of connections or short-circuiting through apparatus. If one could imagine a big building

11

The Sign at Six

like this polarized in some way—anyhow, the electricity is dead. Look here." He pulled an electric flash-light from his pocket. "Bought this fresh on my way here. Tested it, of course. Now, there's nothing wonderful about these toys going back on a man; *but*"—he pressed the button and peered down the lens— "this is a funny coincidence." He turned the lens toward his friend. The filament was dark.

CHAPTER III

THE condition of affairs in the Atlas Building lasted long enough to carry the matter up to the experts in the employ of the companies; that is to say, until about three o'clock the following morning. Then, without reason, and all at once, the whole building from top to bottom was a blaze of incandescent light.

One of the men, stepping to the nearest telephone, unhooked the receiver. To his ear came the low busy hum of a live wire. Somebody touched a bell button, and the head janitor, running joyfully, two steps at a time, from his lair, cried out that his bell had rung.

The little group of workmen and experts

13

The Sign at Six

nodded in a competent and satisfied manner, and began leisurely to pack their tools as though at the successful completion of a long and difficult job.

But every man jack of them knew perfectly well that the electrical apparatus of the building was now in exactly the same condition as it had been the evening before. No repair work had followed a futile investigation.

As the group moved toward the outer air, the head repair man quietly dropped behind. Surreptitiously he applied the slender cords of his pocket ammeter to the zinc and carbon of the dead batteries concerning whose freshness he and his assistant had argued. The delicate needle leaped forward, quivered like a snake's tongue, and hovered over a number.

"Fifteen," read the repair man; and then, after a moment: "Hell!"

The daily business, therefore, opened normally. The elevators shot from floor to floor;

The Sign at Six

the telephones rang; the call-bells buzzed, and all was well. At six o'clock came the scrub-woman; at half past seven the office boys; at eight the clerks; a little later some of the heads; and precisely at nine Malachi McCarthy, as was his invariable habit.

As the bulky form of the political boss pushed around the leaves of the revolving door, the elevator starter glanced at his watch. This was not to determine if McCarthy was on time, but to see if the watch was right.

McCarthy had recovered his good humor. He threw a joke at the negro polishing the brass, and paused genially to exchange a word with the elevator starter.

"Worked until about three o'clock," the latter answered a question. "Got it fixed all right. No, they didn't say what was the matter. Something to do with the wires, I suppose."

"Most like," agreed McCarthy.

The Sign at Six

At this moment an elevator dropped from above and came to rest, like a swift bird alighting. The doors parted to let out a young man wearing the cap of the United Wireless.

"Good morning, Mr. McCarthy," this young man remarked in passing. "Aren't going into the sign-painting business, are you?" He laughed.

"What ye givin' us, Mike?" demanded McCarthy.

The young man wheeled to include the elevator starter in the joke.

"Air was full of dope most of last night from some merry little jester working a toy, home-made. He just kept repeating the same thing—something about 'McCarthy, at six o'clock you shall have a sign given unto you. It works,' over and over all night. Some new advertising dodge, I reckon. Didn't know but you were the McCarthy and were getting a present from some admiring constituent."

The Sign at Six

He threw back his head and laughed, but McCarthy's ready anger rose.

"Where did the stuff come from?"

"Out of the fresh air," replied the operator. "From most anywhere inside the zone of communication."

"Couldn't you tell who sent it?"

"No way. It wasn't signed. Come from quite a distance, though."

"How can you tell that?"

"You can tell by the way it sounds. Say, they ought to be a law about these amatoors cluttering up the air this way. Sometimes I got to pick my own dope out of a dozen or fifteen messages all ticking away in my head-piece at once."

"I know the crazy slob what sent 'em, all right, all right," growled McCarthy. "He's nutty for fair."

"Well, if he's nutty, I wish you'd hurry his little trip to Matteawan," complained the operator, turning away.

17

The Sign at Six

The boss went to his office, where he established himself behind his table-top desk. There all day he conducted a leisurely business of mysterious import, sitting where the cool autumn breeze from the river brought its refreshment. His desk top held no papers; the writing materials lay undisturbed. Sometimes the office contained half a dozen people. Sometimes it was quite empty, and McCarthy sat drumming his blunt fingers on the window-sill, chewing a cigar, and gazing out over the city he owned.

There were two other, inner, offices to McCarthy's establishment, in which sat a private secretary and an office boy. Occasionally McCarthy, with some especial visitor, retired to one of these for a more confidential conversation. The secretary seemed always very busy; the office boy was often in the street. At noon McCarthy took lunch at a small round table in the café below. When he reappeared at the

The Sign at Six

elevator shaft, the elevator starter again verified his watch. Malachi McCarthy had but the one virtue of accuracy, and that had to do with matters of time. At five minutes of six he reached for his hat; at three minutes of six he boarded the elevator.

"Runs all right to-day, Sam," he remarked genially to the boy whom he had half throttled the evening before.

He stood for a moment in the entrance of the building, enjoying the sight of the crowds hurrying to their cars, the elevated, the subway, and the ferries. The clang and roar of the city pleased his senses, as a vessel vibrates to its master tone. McCarthy was feeling largely paternal as he stepped toward the corner, for to a great extent the destinies of these people were in his hands.

"Easy marks!" was his philanthropic expression of this sentiment.

At the corner he stopped for a car. He

The Sign at Six

glanced up at the clock of the Metropolitan tower. The bronze hand pointed to the stroke of six. As he looked, the first note of the quarter chimes rang out. The car swung the corner and headed down the street. Mc-Carthy stepped forward. The sweet chimes ceased their fourfold phrasing, and the great bell began its spaced and solemn booming.

One!—Two!—Three!—Four!—Five!—Six! McCarthy counted. At the recollection of a crazy message from the Unknown, he smiled. He stepped forward to hold up his hand at the car. Somewhat to his surprise the car had already stopped some twenty feet away.

McCarthy picked his way to the car.

"Wonder you wouldn't stop at a crossing," he growled, swinging aboard.

"Juice give out," explained the motorman.

McCarthy clambered aboard and sat down in a comfortably filled car. Up and down the perspective of the street could be seen other

The Sign at Six

cars, also stalled. Ten minutes slipped by; then Malachi McCarthy grew impatient. With a muttered growl he rose, elbowed his way through the strap-hangers, and stepped to the street. A row of idle taxicabs stood in front of the Atlas Building. Into the first of these bounced McCarthy, throwing his address to the expectant chauffeur.

The man hopped down from his box, threw on the coil switch and ran to the front. He turned the engine over the compression, but no explosion followed. He repeated the effort a dozen times. Then, grasping the starting handle with a firmer grip, he "whirled" the engine—without result.

"What's the matter? Can't you make her go?" demanded McCarthy, thrusting his head from the door.

"Will you please listen, sir, and see if you hear a buzz when I turn her over?" requested the chauffeur.

The Sign at Six

"I don't hear nothing," was the verdict.

"I'm sorry, but you'll have to take another cab," then said the man. "My coil's gone back on me."

McCarthy impatiently descended, entered the next taxi in line, and repeated the same experience. By now the other chauffeurs, noticing the predicament of their brethren, were anxiously and perspiringly at work. Not an engine answered the call of the road! A passing truck driver, grinning from ear to ear, drove slowly down the line, dealing out the ancient jests rescued for the occasion from an oblivion to which the perfection of the automobile had consigned them.

McCarthy added his mite; he was beginning to feel himself the victim of a series of nagging impertinences, which he resented after his kind.

"If," said he, "your company would put out something on the street besides a bunch of retired grist-mills with clock dials hitched on to

The Sign at Six

them, you might be able to give the public some service. I've got lots of time. Don't hurry through your afternoon exercise on my account. Just buy a lawn-mower and a chatelaine watch apiece—you'd do just as well."

By now every man had his battery box open. McCarthy left them, puzzling over the singular failure of the electrical apparatus, which is the nervous system of the modern automobile.

He turned into Fifth Avenue. An astonishing sight met his eyes.

The old days had returned. The center of the long roadway, down which ordinarily a long file of the purring monsters of gasoline creep and dash, shouldering aside the few hansoms and victorias remaining from a bygone age, now showed but a swinging slashing trot of horses.

Hansoms, hacks, broughams; up-raised whips, whirling in signal; the spat spat of horses' hoofs; all the obsolescent vehicles that

The Sign at Six

ordinarily doze in hope along the stands of the side streets; it was a gay sight of the past raised again for the moment to reality by the same mysterious blight that had shadowed the Atlas Building the night before.

Along the curbs, where they had been hand-pushed under direction from the traffic squad, stood an unbroken line of automobiles. And the hood of each was raised for the eager tinkering of its chauffeur. Past them streamed the horses, and the faces of their drivers were illumined by broad grins.

McCarthy looked about him for a hansom. There was none unengaged. In fact, the boss soon determined that many others, like himself, were waiting for a chance at the first vacant one. Reluctantly he made up his mind to walk. He glanced up at the tower of the Metropolitan Building; then stared in astonishment. The hands of the great dial were still perpendicular —the hour indicated was still six o'clock!

CHAPTER IV

DARKNESS AND PANIC

PROBABLY the only men in the whole of New York who accepted promptly and unquestioningly the fact that the entire electrical apparatus of the city was paralyzed were those in the newspaper offices. These capable citizens, accustomed to quick adaptations to new environments and to wide reaches of the imagination, made two or three experiments, and accepted the inevitable.

Within ten minutes the *Despatch* had messenger boys on tap instead of bells, bicycles instead of telephones, and a variety of lamps and candles in place of electricity. Everybody else in town was speculating why in blazes this vis-

The Sign at Six

itation had struck them.   The *Despatch* was
out after news.

Marsden, city editor, detailed three men to
dig up expert opinion on *why* it had all happened.

"And if the scientific men haven't any other
notions, ask 'em if it's anything to do with the
earth passing through the tail of the comet,"
he told them.

The rest of the staff he turned out for stories
of the effects.   His imagination was struck by
the contemplation of a modern civilized city
deprived of its nerve system.

"Hunt up the little stuff," said he; "the big
stuff will hunt you up—if you scatter."

After covering the usual police-station, theater and hotel assignments, he sent Hallowell
to the bridge; Longman to the Grand Central;
Kennedy, Warren and Thomas to the tubes,
subways and ferries.   The others he told to go
out on the streets.

The Sign at Six

They saw a city of four million people stopped short on its way home to dinner! They saw a city, miles in extent, set back without preparation to a communication by messenger only! They saw a city, unprepared, blinking its way by the inadequate illuminations of a half-century gone by!

Hallowell found a packed mass of humanity at the bridge. Where ordinarily is a crush, even with incessant outgoing trains sucking away at the surplus, now was a panic—a panic the more terrible in that it was solid, sullen, inert, motionless. Women fainted, and stood unconscious, erect. Men sank slowly from sight, agonized, their faces contorted, but unheard in the dull roar of the crowd, and were seen no more. Around the edges people fought frantically to get out; and others, with the blind, unreasoning, home instinct, fought as hard to get in.

The police were unavailing. They could not

The Sign at Six

penetrate to break the center. Across the bridge streamed a procession of bruised and battered humanity, escaped from or cast forth by the maelstrom. The daylight was fading, and within the sheds men could not see one another's faces.

Longman at the Grand Central observed a large and curious crowd that filled the building and packed the streets round about. They waited for their trains, and the twilight gathered. For ten minutes trains continued to enter the shed. This puzzled Longman until he remembered that gravity would bring in those this side of Harlem. None went out. The waiting throng was a hotbed for rumors. Longman collected much human-interest stuff, and was quite well satisfied with his story—until he saw what it had meant elsewhere.

For in the subways and tubes the stoppage of the trains had automatically discontinued the suction ventilation. The underground

The Sign at Six

thousands, in mortal terror of the non-existent third-rail danger, groped their way painfully to the stations. With inconceivable swiftness the mephitic vapors gathered. Strong men staggered fainting into the streets. When revived they told dreadful tales of stumbling over windrows of bodies there below.

Through the gathering twilight of the streets, dusky and shadowy, flitted bat-like the criminals of the underworld. What they saw, that they took. Growing bolder, they progressed from pocket-picking to holdups, from holdups to looting. The police reserves were all out; they could do little. Favored by obscurity, the thieves plundered. It would have needed a solid cordon of officers to have protected adequately the retail district. Swiftly a guerrilla warfare sprang up. Bullets whistled. Anarchy raised its snaky locks and peered red-eyed through the darkened streets of the city

Here and there fire broke out. Men on bi-

The Sign at Six

cycles brought in the alarms; then, as twilight thickened, men on foot. Chief Croker promptly established lookouts in all the tall towers, as watchmen used a hundred years ago to watch the night.

And, up-town, Smith cursed the necessity of reading his evening paper by candle-light; and Mary, the cook, grumbled because she could not telephone the grocery for some forgotten ingredient; and Jones' dinner party was very hilarious over the joke on their host; and men swore and their wives worried because they had perforce to be very late to dinner.

At eight o'clock, two hours after the inception of the curious phenomena, the condition suddenly passed. The intimation came to the various parts of the city in different ways. Strangely enough, only gradually did the lights and transportation facilities resume their functions. Most of the dynamos were being inspected by puzzled experts. Here and there

The Sign at Six

the blazing of a group of lights, the ringing of a bell, the response of a volt or ammeter to test, hinted to the masters of the lightnings that their rebellious steeds again answered the bit.

Within a half-hour the city's illuminations again reflected softly from the haze of the autumn sky; the clang of the merry trolley, the wail of the motor's siren again smote the air.

Malachi McCarthy, having caught a ride on a friendly dray, arrived home. At eight ten his telephone bell for the first time jangled its summons. McCarthy answered it.

"I'm Simmons, the wireless operator," the small voice told him. "Say! There's a lot of these fool messages in the air again. You know what they said last night about six o'clock, and what happened."

"Let's have 'em," growled McCarthy.

"Here she is: 'McCarthy, will you do as I tell you? Answer. Remember the sign at six o'clock.' It's signed 'M.'"

The Sign at Six

"Where did that come from?" asked the boss.

"Can't tell, but somewheres a long ways off."

"How do you know that?"

"By the sound."

"How far—about?"

"Might be anywhere."

"Can you get an answer back?"

"I think so. Can't tell whether my spark will reach that far. I can send out a call for 'M.'"

"Well, send this," said McCarthy. "'Go to hell.'"

On the evening of the phenomena afore mentioned, Percy Darrow had returned to his apartments, where he had dressed unusually early, and by daylight. This was because he had a dinner engagement up-town. It was an informal engagement for a family dinner at seven o'clock; but Percy had been requested by one of the members to come at about six.

The Sign at Six

This was because the other members would presumably be dressing between six and seven.

The young man found a fire blazing on the hearth, although the evening was warm. A graceful girl sat looking into the flames. She did not rise as the scientist entered, but held out her hand with an air of engaging frankness.

"Sit down," she invited the guest. "This is a fearful and wonderful time to ask you to venture abroad in your dress clothes, but I wanted to see you most particularly before the rest of the family comes down."

"You are a singularly beautiful woman," observed Darrow in a detached manner, as he disposed his long form gracefully in the opposite armchair.

The girl looked at him sharply.

"That is intended as an excuse or explanation—not in the least as a compliment," Darrow went on.

The Sign at Six

"You would not be so obliging, if I were not—beautiful?" shot back the girl. "That is indeed not complimentary!"

"I should be exactly as obliging," amended Darrow lazily, "but I should not feel so generally satisfied and pleased and rewarded in advance. I should have more of a feeling of virtue, and less of one of pleasure."

"I see," said the girl, her brows still level. "Then I suppose you are not interested in what I might ask you as one human being to another!"

"Pardon me, Helen," interrupted Darrow, with unusual decision. "That is just what I am interested in—you as a human being, a delicious, beautiful, feminine, human being who could mean half the created universe to a lucky man."

"But not the whole—"

"No, not the whole," mused Darrow, relaxing to his old indolent attitude. "You see,"

34

The Sign at Six

he roused himself to explain, "I am a scientist, for instance. You could not be a scientist; you have not the training."

"Nor the brains," interposed Helen Warford, a trifle bitterly.

"Nor the kind of brains," amended Darrow. "I have enough of that sort myself," he added. He leaned forward, a hunger leaping in the depths of his brown eyes. "Helen," he pleaded, "can't you see how we need each other?"

But the girl shut both her eyes, and shook her head vigorously.

"Unless people can be *everything* to each other, they should be nothing—people like us," said she.

Darrow sighed and leaned back.

"I feel that way, but the devil of it is I can't think it," said he. Then after a pause: "What is it you want of me, Helen? I'm ready."

She sat up straight, and clasped her hands.

The Sign at Six

"It's Jack," said she.

"What's the matter with Jack?"

"Everything—and nothing. He's just out of college. This fall he must go to work. Father wants him to go into an office. Jack doesn't care much, and will drift into the office unless somebody stops him."

"Well?" said Darrow.

"An office will ruin him. He isn't in the least interested in the things they do in offices; and he's too high-spirited to settle down to a grind."

"He's like you in spirit, Helen," said Darrow. "What is he interested in?"

"He's interested in you."

"What!" cried Darrow. "Wish it were a family trait."

"He thinks you are wonderful, and he knows all about all your adventures and voyages with Doctor Schermerhorn. He admires the way you look and act and talk. I suspect him of

36

"Can't you see how we need each other?"

The Sign at Six

trying to imitate you." Helen's eyes gleamed with amusement.

Darrow smiled his slow and languid smile.

"The last time I saw Jack he stood six feet and weighed about one hundred and eight-five pounds," he pointed out.

"The imitation is funny," admitted Helen, "but based on genuine admiration."

"What do you want me to do with him?" drawled Darrow.

"I thought you could take him in with you; get him started at something scientific; something that would interest and absorb him, and something that would not leave all his real energies free for mischief."

Darrow leaned his head against the back of the chair and laughed softly. So long did his amusement continue that Helen at length brought him rather sharply to account.

"I was merely admiring," then exclaimed Darrow, "the delicious femininity of the proposal. It displays at once such really remarkable insight into the psychological needs of another human being, and such abysmal ignorance of the demands of what we are pleased to call science."

"You are the most superior and exasperating and conceited man I know!" cried Helen. "I am sorry I asked you. I'd like to know what there is so silly in my remarks!"

"Jack is physically very strong; he is most courageous; he has a good disposition, a gentleman's code, and an eager likable nature. I gather further that he does me the honor of admiring me personally. He has received a general, not a special, college education."

"Well!" challenged Helen.

"Barring the last, these are exactly the qualifications of a good bull-terrier."

"Oh!" cried the girl indignantly, and half rising. "You are insulting!"

"No," denied Darrow. "Not that—never

The Sign at Six

to you, Helen, and you know it! I'm merely
talking sense. Leaving aside the minor consideration that I am myself looking for em-
ployment, what use has a scientist for a bull-
terrier? Jack has no aptitude for science; he
has had none of the accurate training absolutely essential to science. He probably
wouldn't be interested in science. At the moment he happens to admire me, and I'm mighty
glad and proud that it is so. But that doesn't
help. If I happened to be a saloon man, Jack
would quite as cheerfully want to be a bar-
keeper. I'd do anything in the world to help
Jack; but I'm not the man. You want to hunt
up somebody that needs a good bull-terrier.
Lots do."

"I hate such a cold-blooded way of going
at things!" cried the girl. "You show no more
interest in Jack than if—than if—"

Darrow smiled whimsically. "Indeed I do,
Helen," he said quietly; "that is why I don't

The Sign at Six

want to touch his life. Science would ruin
him quicker than an office—in the long run.
What he wants is a job of action—something
out West—or in the construction of our great
and good city. Now, if I had a political pull,
instead of a scientific twist, I could land Jack
in a minute. Why don't you try that?"

But Helen slowly shook her head.

"Father and McCarthy are enemies," she
said simply. She arose with an air of weari-
ness. "How dark it's getting!" she said, and
pressed the electric button in the wall.

The light did not respond.

"That's queer," she remarked, and pulled
the chain that controlled the reading light on
the table. That, too, failed to illuminate.
"Something must be wrong with those things
at the meter—what do you call them?"

"Fuses," suggested Darrow.

"Yes, that's it. I'll ring and have Blake
screw in another."

The Sign at Six

Darrow was staring at a small object he had taken from his pocket. It was the electric flash-light he habitually carried to light his way up the three dark flights at his lodgings.

"Let me call him for you," he suggested, rising.

"I'll ring," said Helen.

But Darrow was already in the hall.

"Blake!" he called down the basement stairway. "Bring lamps—or candles."

The man appeared on the word, carrying a lamp.

"I already had this, sir," he explained. "The lights went out some time ago."

"Did you look at the—fuses?" asked Helen.

"Yes, miss."

"Well, telephone to the electric company at once. We must have light."

Percy Darrow had taken his place again in the armchair by the fire.

"It is useless," said he, quietly.

The Sign at Six

"Useless!" echoed Helen. "What do you mean?" Blake stood quietly at attention.

"You will find your telephone also out of order."

Helen darted from the room, only to return after a moment, laughing.

"You are a true wizard," she said. "Tell me, how did you know? What has happened?"

"A city," stated Percy didactically, "is like a mollusk; it depends largely for its life and health on the artificial shell it has constructed. Unless I am very much mistaken, this particular mollusk is going to get a chance to try life without its shell."

"I don't understand you," said Helen.

"You will," said Percy Darrow.

Mr. and Mrs. Warford descended soon after. They sat down to dinner by the light of the table candles only. Darrow hardly joined at all in the talk, but sat lost in a brown study,

The Sign at Six

from which he only roused sufficiently to accept or refuse the dishes offered him. At about eight o'clock the telephone bell clicked a single stroke, as though the circuit had been closed. At the sound Darrow started, then reached swiftly into his pocket for his little flash-light. He gravely pressed the button of this; then abruptly rose.

"I must use your telphone," said he, without apology.

He was gone barely a minute; then returned to the table with a clouded brow. Almost immediately after the company had arisen from the board, he excused himself and left.

After he had assumed his coat, however, he returned for a final word with Helen.

"Where is Jack this evening?" he asked.

"Dining out with friends. Why?"

"Will you see him to-night?"

"I can if necessary."

"Do. Tell him to come down to my room

as near eight o'clock to-morrow morning as he can. I've changed my mind."

"Oh!" cried Helen joyously. "Then you've concluded I'm right, after all?"

"No," said Darrow; "but if this thing carries out to its logical conclusion, I'm going to need a good bull-terrier pup!"

CHAPTER V

A SCIENTIST IN PINK SILK

THE next morning promptly at eight o'clock Jack Warford, in response to a muttered invitation, burst excitedly into Percy Darrow's room. He found the scientist, draped in a pale-pink silk kimono embroidered with light-blue butterflies, scraping methodically at his face with a safety-razor. At the sight the young fellow came to an abrupt stop, as though some one had met him with a dash of cold water in the face.

"Hello!" said he, in a constrained voice. "Just up?"

Darrow cast a glance through his long silky lashes at the newcomer.

45

The Sign at Six

"Yes, my amiable young canine, just up."

Jack looked somewhat puzzled at the appellation, but seated himself.

"Helen said you wanted to see me," he suggested.

Darrow leisurely cleaned the component parts of his safety-razor, washed and anointed his face, and turned.

"I do," said he, "if you're game."

"Of course I'm game!" cried the boy indignantly.

Darrow surveyed his fresh, young, eager face and the trim taut bulk of him with dispassionate eyes.

"Are you?" he remarked simply. "Possibly. But you're not the man to be sure of it."

"I didn't mean it as bragging," cried Jack, flushing.

"Surely not," drawled Darrow, stretching out his long legs. "But no man can tell whether or not he's game until he's tried out.

46

The Sign at Six

That's no reflection on him, either. I remember once I went through seeing my best friend murdered; being shot at a dozen times myself as I climbed a cliff; seeing a pirate ship destroyed with all on board, apparently by the hand of Providence; escaping from a big volcanic bust-up into a cave, and having the cave entrance drop down shut behind me. I was as cool as a cucumber all through it. I remember congratulating myself that, anyhow, I was going to die game."

"By Jove!" murmured Jack Warford, staring at him, fascinated. Evidently, the super-beautiful garment had been forgotten.

"Then a war-ship's crew rescued me; and I broke down completely, and acted like a silly ass. I wasn't game at all; I'd just managed to postpone finding it out for a while."

"It was just the reaction!" cried Jack.

"Well, if that sort of reaction happens along before the trouble is all over, it looks uncommonly like loss of nerve," Percy Darrow pointed out. "No man knows whether or not he's game," he repeated. "However," he smiled whimsically, "I imagine you're likely to postpone your reactions as well as the next."

"What's up? What do you want me to do?"

"Stick by me; obey orders," said Darrow.

"What's up?"

"Did you notice anything in the papers this morning?"

"They're full of this electrical failure last night. Haven't you seen them?"

"Not yet. While I dress, tell me what they say."

"The worst was in the tubes—" Warford began, but Darrow interrupted him.

"I could tell you exactly what must have happened," said he, "if the failure was complete. Never mind that. Was the condition general, or only local? How far did it extend?"

The Sign at Six

"It seemed to be confined to New York, and only about to Highbridge."

"Long Island? Jersey?"

"Yes; it hit them, too."

"What are the theories?"

"I couldn't see that they had any—that I could understand," said Jack. "There's some talk of the influence of a comet."

"Rubbish! Who sprung that?"

"Professor Aitken, I think."

"He ought to know better. Any others?"

"I couldn't understand them all. There was one of polarizing the island because of the steel structures; and the—"

"No human agency?"

"What?"

"No man or men are suspected of bringing this about?"

"Oh, no! You don't think—"

"No, I don't think. I only imagine; and I haven't much basis for imagining. But if my

imaginations come out right, we'll have plenty
to do."

"Where, now?" asked Jack, as the scientist
finished dressing and reached for his hat.
"Breakfast?"

"No, I ate that before I dressed. We'll
make a call on the Atlas Building."

"All right," agreed Jack cheerfully. "What
for?"

"To ask McCarthy if he hasn't a job for
you in construction."

Jack came to a dead halt.

"Say!" he cried. "Look here! You don't
quite get the humor of that. Why, McCarthy
loves the name of Warford about the way a
yellow dog loves a tin can to his tail."

"We'll call on him, just the same," insisted
Darrow.

"I'm game," said Jack, "but I can tell you
the answer right now. No need to walk to
the Atlas Building."

The Sign at Six

"I have a notion the Atlas Building is going to be a mighty interesting place," said Darrow.

They debouched on the street. The air was soft and golden; the sun warm with the Indian summer. The clock on the Metropolitan tower was booming nine. As the two set out at a slow saunter down the backwater of the side street, Darrow explained a little further.

"Jack," said he abruptly, "I'll tell you what I think—or imagine. I believe last night's phenomena were controlled, not fortuitous or the result of natural forces. In other words, some man turned off the juice in this city; and turned it on again. How he did it, I do not know; but he did it very completely. It was not a question of wiring alone. Even dry-cell batteries were affected. Now, I can think of only one broad general principle by which he could accomplish that result. Just what means he took to apply the principle is beyond my knowledge. But if I am correct in my supposition, there occurs to me no reason why he should not go a step or so farther."

"I don't believe I follow," said Jack contritely.

"What I'm driving at is this," said Darrow; "this is not the end of the circus by any means. We're going to see a lot of funny things—if my guess is anywhere near right."

CHAPTER VI

THE WRATH TO COME

"DID you ever meet McCarthy?" asked Darrow, as the elevator of the Atlas sprang upward.

"Never."

"Well, no matter what he says or does, I want you to say nothing—nothing."

"Correct," said Jack. "I'll down-charge."

"That's right," Darrow approved. "First of all, wait outside until I call you."

McCarthy was already at his desk, and in evil humor. When Darrow entered, he merely looked up and growled.

"Good morning," Darrow greeted him easily. "Any wireless this morning?"

The Sign at Six

McCarthy threw back his heavy head.

"That damn operator's been leaking!" he cried.

"So there are 'wireless'," observed Darrow. "No, your operator didn't leak. Who is he?"

"If he didn't leak, what did you say that for?"

"I'm a good guesser," replied Darrow enigmatically. "They say anything about a 'sign' being sent, and such talk?"

"You've been gettin' the dope yourself out of the air," returned McCarthy sullenly.

"Look here, my fat friend," drawled Darrow, his eyes half closing, "I'm getting nothing from anywhere except in my own gray matter. What do your messages have to say?"

"Why should I tell you?"

"Because I'm interested—and because I know who sent 'em."

"So do I," snarled McCarthy, in a gust of temper.

54

The Sign at Six

"And I'm beginning to suspect he's a man to look out for. And I doubt if you'll ever find him. Of course, he's responsible for the row last night—as well as for the trouble in the Atlas Building the night before."

"I don't know whether he is or not."

"Oh, yes, you do; and I do; and the wireless man does. We're the only three. The rest of them are still figuring on comets."

"Well?"

"I don't suppose there's any real doubt left in your mind but that this man can turn the juice off again, if he wants to?"

"I don't know as he did it," persisted McCarthy stoutly.

"Now, how **long** do you suppose you'd last if the public should get on to the fact that this hidden power was going to exert itself again unless you left town?"

A slight moisture bedewed McCarthy's forehead.

The Sign at Six

"Not all your police, nor all your power could save you, if the general public once became thoroughly convinced that it was to go through another experience like last night's unless it ousted you. Why, a mob of a million men would gather against you in an hour. You see," drawled Percy Darrow, "why you'd better look after that wireless man of yours— and me."

"And you," repeated McCarthy. "What do you want?"

"I want to see those wireless messages, first of all," said Darrow, reaching out his hand.

McCarthy hesitated; then swiftly thrust forward the flimsies. Darrow, a slight smile curving his full red lips, held them to the light. They read as follows:

"McCarthy: A sign was promised you at six o'clock. It has been sent. Repent and beware! Go while there is yet time.   M."

The Sign at Six

There were four of these, couched in almost identical language. The fifth and last message was shorter:

"McCARTHY: Flee from the wrath to come.
"M."

"What," said Darrow, "is to prevent the other operators who must have caught this message from giving it to the public? What, indeed, is to prevent M.'s appealing direct to the public?"

"I don't know," confessed McCarthy miserably. "Do you?"

"Not at this moment. Will you send for the operator who took these?"

McCarthy snatched down the telephone receiver, through which presently he spoke a message.

"What have you got to do with this?" he demanded, after he had hung up the hook.

"I want something," said Percy, "of course."

The Sign at Six

"Sure," growled McCarthy, once more back on familiar ground, and glad of it. "What is it?"

"I'll tell you when I'm sure whether I can do anything for you in this matter."

"If this fellow didn't leak, how did you know about them wireless?" demanded McCarthy again. "How do you know who's doin' this?"

Darrow smiled.

"The man who can control the juice as this man has is a scientific expert with a full scientific equipment. If he communicated at all, it would be by wireless, as that is the easiest way to cover his trail. I remembered your telephone message from the fanatic about sending a 'sign'. Immediately after, the Atlas Building experienced on a small scale what next day the city experienced on a larger scale. It was legitimate inference to connect one with the other. Of course, if our telephone friend

The Sign at Six

was the man who had brought these things about, he had done it to force you to do what he demanded. But he would lose the effect of his lesson unless you understood his connection with the matter. Hence, I concluded that you must have received messages—by wireless—and that they must have repeated the warning as to a 'sign' being sent. It was very simple."

"You're smart, all right," conceded McCarthy.

After a moment the wireless operator came in.

"Simmons," said McCarthy, "answer this man's questions."

"They will be in regard to these messages," said Darrow. "Where are they from?"

"Somewhere in the one-hundred to two-hundred-mile circles, depending on the power of the sending instrument," replied the operator promptly.

The Sign at Six

"Are you sure?"

"I know my instruments pretty well; and I've had experience enough so I can tell by the sound of the sending about how far off they come from."

"And this was from somewhere about one to two hundred miles away, you think?"

"Yes, sir."

"Do you know whether any other instruments caught this?"

"No, only mine." He was very positive.

"How do you know?"

"Mr. McCarthy had me inquire."

"How do you account for it?"

"I don't know, except that maybe my instrument happened to be just tuned to catch it. That's another reason I know it was from far off. The farther away the sending instrument, the nearer exactly it has to be tuned to the receiving instrument. If it was nearer, 'most anybody'd get it."

The Sign at Six

Percy Darrow nodded.

"That's all, I guess. No, hold on. Did any of these come between six and eight last evening?"

For the first time the operator smiled.

"No, sir; my instrument was dead."

He went out.

"Well?" growled McCarthy.

"I don't know; but I can see more trouble."

"Let him turn off his juice," blustered the boss; "we'll be ready, next time."

Percy Darrow smiled.

"Will you?" he contented himself by saying. Then, after a moment's pause, he added, "I'll agree to stop this fellow if you'll give me an absolutely free hand. I'll even agree to find him."

"What do you want?"

"I want a job, a good engineering-construction job, for a friend of mine."

"What can he do?"

The Sign at Six

"He can learn. I want a good honest place where he can learn under a good man."

"Who is he?"

"I'll bring him in."

A moment later Jack, in answer to a summons, entered the office.

McCarthy stared at him. "What kind of a job?" he growled.

"Something active and out of doors," Darrow answered for him; "streets, water, engineering."

"It's a holdup," said McCarthy sullenly drawing a tablet toward himself, and thrusting the stub of a pencil into his mouth.

"A beneficent and just holdup," added Darrow; "the first of its kind in this city."

McCarthy glared at him malevolently.

"It don't go unless you deliver the goods," he threatened.

"Understood," agreed Darrow.

"What's his name?" demanded McCarthy,

The Sign at Six

withdrawing the pencil stub, and preparing to write.

"His name," answered Darrow, "is John Warford, Junior."

McCarthy started to his feet with a bellow of rage, his face turning purple.

"Of all the infernal—!" he roared, and stopped, as though stricken dumb. For two or three words further his mouth and throat went through the motions of speech. Then an expression of mingled fear and astonishment overspread his countenance. He sank back into his chair. Percy Darrow nodded twice and smiled.

CHAPTER VII

A WORLD OF GHOSTS

A DEATHLY stillness had all at once fallen like a blanket, blotting out McCarthy's violent speech. The rattling typewriter in the next room was abruptly stilled. The roar of the city died as a living creature is cut by the sword—all at once, without the transitionary running down of most silences. Absolute dense stillness, like that of a sea calm at night, took the place of the customary city noises. In his astonishment McCarthy thrust a heavy inkstand off the edge of his desk.. It hit the floor, spilled, rolled away; but noiselessly, as would the inkstand in a moving picture.

64

The Sign at Six

To have one's world thus suddenly stricken dumb, to be transported orally from the roar of a city to the peace of a woodland or a becalmed sea is certainly astonishing enough.

But this silence was particularly terrifying to both McCarthy and Jack Warford, though neither would have been able to analyze the reason for its weirdness. For silence is in reality a composite of many lesser noises. In a woodland almost inaudible insects hum, breezes blow, leaves and grasses rustle; at sea the tiny waves lap the sides and equally tiny breaths of air stir the cordage; within the confines of the human shell the mere physical acts of breathing, swallowing, winking, the mere physical facts of the circulation of the blood, the beating of the heart, produce each its sound.

Even a man totally deaf feels the subtle influence of these latter physical phenomena. And underneath all sound, perceptible alike to those who can hear and those who can not, are

The Sign at Six

the vibrations that accompany every activity
of nature as the manifestations of motion or
of life. An ordinary deep silence is not so
much an absence of sound as an absence of
accustomed or loud sound. And in that unusual hush often for the first time a man becomes acutely aware of the singing of the
blood in his ears.

But this silence was absolute. All these minor sounds had been eliminated.

For a moment Boss McCarthy stared; then
shoved back his chair with a violent motion,
and rose. He was like a shadow on a screen.
The filching from the world of one element of
its every-day life had unexpectedly rendered it
all phantasmagoric.

As McCarthy shouted, and no sound came;
as he moved from behind his desk, and no jar
accompanied his heavy footfall, he appeared
to lose blood and substance, to become unreal.
As no sound issued from his contorted face,

The Sign at Six

so it seemed that no force would follow his blow, were he to deliver one.

He stumbled forward, dazed and groping as though he were in the dark, instead of merely in silence; a striking example in the uncertainty of his movements of how closely our senses depend on one another.

Jack spoke twice, then closed his lips in a grim straight line. He held his elbows close to his sides, and looked ready for anything.

A look of mild triumph illumined Percy Darrow's usually languid countenance. He stepped quickly to the wall, and turned the button of the incandescent globe. The light instantly glowed. At this he nodded twice more. From his pocket he drew a note-book and pencil, wrote in it a few words, and handed it to the dazed and uncertain boss.

"I was right," Darrow had scrawled. "This proves it. It's by no means the end. Better be good."

The Sign at Six

McCarthy's bulldog courage had recovered from its first daze. He began to see that this visitation was not entirely personal, but extended also to his two companions. This relieved his mind, for he had suspected some strange new apoplexy.

"Did you expect this?" he wrote.

Darrow nodded.

Together the three ghosts left the phantom office, and glided down the phantom halls. Other ghosts in various stages of alarm were already making their way down the stairs. Some of them spoke, but no sound came. One woman, her eyes frightened, reached out furtively to touch her neighbor, apparently to assure herself of his reality. Urged by an uncontrollable impulse, a man thrust his hand through the ground glass of an office door. The glass shivered, and crashed to the tile floor. The pieces broke—silently. It was as though the man had been the figure in a cinemato-

The Sign at Six

graph illusion. He stared at his cut and bleeding hand. The woman who had touched the man suddenly threw back her head and screamed. They could see her eyes roll back, her face change color, could discern the straining of her throat. No sound came.

At this a panic seized them. They rushed down the stairs, clambering over one another, pushing, scrambling, falling. A mob of a hundred men fought for precedence. Blows were struck. No faintest murmur of tumult came from their futile heat. It might have been the riot of a wax-works in a vacuum.

They fell into the lower hallway, and fought their way to the street, and stood there dazed and staring, a strange, wild-eyed, white-faced, bloody crew. The hurrying avenue stopped to gaze on them curiously, gathering compact in a mob that blocked all traffic. Policemen pushed their way in and began roughly to question—and to question in real audible words.

The Sign at Six

But for the space of a full minute these people stood there staring upward, drinking in the blessed sound that poured in on them lavishly from the life of the street; drinking deep gulps of air, as though air had lacked.

Darrow, and with him Jack Warford, had descended more leisurely. Before leaving the building Darrow placed the flat of his hands over his ears, and motioned Jack to do the same. Thus they missed the stunning effect of receiving the world of noise all at once; as a man goes to a bright light from a dark room. Furthermore, Darrow returned several times from the sound to the silence, trying to determine where the line of demarcation was drawn. Then, motioning to Jack, he began methodically to make his way through the crowd.

This proved to be by no means an easy task. Rumors of all sorts were afoot. Some bold spirits were testing a new sensation by ventur-

The Sign at Six

ing into the corridor of the building. The police were undecided as to what should be done. One or two reporters were already at hand, investigating. McCarthy, his assurance returned, was conversing earnestly with a police captain.

Percy Darrow, closely followed by Jack, managed to worm his way through the crowd, and finally debouched on Broadway.

"What was it? What struck us?" demanded Jack. "Do you know?"

"I can guess; in essence," said Percy. "I was pretty sure after last evening's trouble; but this underscores it, proves it. Also, it opens the way."

"What do you mean?"

"Along the lines of these phenomena there are two more things possible. Possible, I say. They might be called certain, were we dealing only with theory; but there is still some doubt how the practical side of it may work out."

The Sign at Six

"I suppose you know what you're talking about," said Jack resignedly. "I don't."

"You don't need to, yet. But here's what I mean. If my theory is correct, we are likely to be surprised still further."

Jack ruminated; then his engaging young face lighted up with a smile.

"All right," said he; "I'm enlisted for the war. What have you got to do with it?"

"I'll explain this much," said Darrow; "more I'll not tell at present, even to you. If one breath should get out that any one suspected—well, this is a man-hunt."

"Who's the man?"

"An enemy of McCarthy."

"Whom you are going to find for him?"

"Perhaps."

"And you were putting up that job for me as part of your pay!"

Percy Darrow smiled slowly.

The Sign at Six

"As all of my pay—from McCarthy," said he. "I was just bedeviling him."

Jack Warford started to say something, but the scientist cut him short.

"This is bigger than McCarthy," he said decisively. "We are the only people in this city who suspect a human origin of these phenomena. Other men are yet working, and will continue to work, on the supposition that they are the results of some unbalanced natural conditions. The phenomena are, as yet, harmless. It will not greatly injure the city, once it is prepared, to be without electricity or without sound for limited periods. I doubt very much whether the Unknown can continue these phenomena for longer than limited periods. But conceivably this man may become a peril. He has, if I reason correctly, four arrows in his quiver; the fourth is dangerous. It is our duty to find him before he uses the fourth arrow—if

The Sign at Six

indeed he has discovered the method of doing so. That is always in doubt."

Jack's eyes were shining.

"Bully!" he cried.

"He may conceivably possess the power to launch the fourth and dangerous arrow, but may withhold it unless he believes himself suspected or close pressed. His probable mental processes are obscure. At present he directs himself solely against McCarthy." Percy Darrow had been thinking aloud, and realized it with a smile. "This is one of your jobs, fellow detective," said he. "You've got to be a mark for me to think at."

"I wish you'd think a little more clearly," observed Jack. "It sounds interesting, but jumbled. I feel the way I did when I began to read Greek."

"McCarthy's incidental," observed Darrow in his detached tone.

"Eh?"

The Sign at Six

"Oh, I thought we might as well worry Mc-Carthy by asking him for that job on the side. It's amusing."

"What do you want me to do?" asked Jack.

"This," said Darrow, with an unusual rapidity of utterance. "See that thick-set, quick man in gray clothes? He's a policeman. In a moment he'll arrest me."

"Arrest you—why?" demanded Jack, in tones of great astonishment.

"I reason that McCarthy will come to that conclusion. He is beginning to think I have something to do with what he calls his annoyances. I saw it in his eyes. This last curious manifestation came along too pat. You remember, it cut off the dressing-down he was going to give me." Darrow chuckled in appreciation. "Didn't the humor of that strike you?"

"Me? Oh, I was scared," admitted Jack.

"I want you to go home and tell Helen just

75

The Sign at Six

what happened in the Atlas Building. Do not tell her that I believe the phenomena are due to any human agency. Say simply that if it is repeated, and she happens to be within the zone of its influence, to keep calm, and wait. It will pass, and it is not to be feared. Tell her I said so."

"Lord!" cried Jack. "You don't think it's going to happen again!"

"Within the next twenty-four hours," said Darrow.

"Oughtn't we to warn the people?"

"And let our hidden antagonist know we are aware of his existence?" inquired Darrow.

"Anything else?"

"No—yes. Buy a gun. If I bring you into any trouble, I'll see you clear. You understand?"

"I do."

"I rely on your being game."

"To the limit," said Jack. "Here comes

your friend. Won't this arrest ball things up?
Shall I rustle bail?"

"No," said Darrow. "I want to think. All
I need is all the papers. I'll be out by ten to-
morrow morning, sure."

"Why are you sure of that?"

*"Because by that hour McCarthy will have
disappeared,"* said Percy Darrow.

The man in the gray suit, having finished
his scrutiny, lounged forward.

"You are Mr. Darrow," he stated.

"Sure I am, my amiable but obvious sleuth,"
drawled that young man. "Lead on." He
nodded a farewell to Jack, and linked his arm
in that of the officer. After a few moments
he burst into an irrepressible chuckle.

"The fat, thick-necked, thick-witted, old
fool!" said he.

CHAPTER VIII

PERCY DARROW'S THEORY

PERCY DARROW in the police station, where he had been assigned an unused office instead of a cell, amused himself reading the newspapers, of which he caused to be brought in a full supply. Theories had begun to claim their share of the space which, up to now, the fact stories had completely monopolized. Darrow, his feet up, a cigarette depending from one corner of his mouth, read them through to the end. Then he indulged the white walls of his little apartment with one of his slow smiles. The simplest of the theories had to do with comets. The most elaborate traced out an analogy between the "blind

78

The Sign at Six

spot" in vision and a "point of rest" in physical manifestations—this "point of rest" had just now happened to drift to a crowded center, and so became manifest.

"Ingenious but fantastic youth," was Percy Darrow's tribute to the author, Professor Eldridge of the university.

The "human-interest" stories of both the evening before and those in the extras describing the latest freak in the Atlas Building, Darrow passed over with barely a glance. But certain figures he copied carefully into his notebook. When he had found all of these, and had transcribed them, they appeared about as follows:

Atlas—Wednesday, 5:25. 3:00 (about) : 9 hr. 35 min.

General—Thursday, 6:00. 7:56 (exact) : 1 hr. 56 min.

Atlas—Friday, 10:10. 10:48 (exact) : 38 min.

The Sign at Six

On the basis of these latter figures he made some calculations which, when finished, he looked on with doubtful satisfaction.

"Need more statistics," said he to himself, "before I can pose as a prophet. Just now I'm merely a guesser."

By now it was afternoon. An official came to announce visitors, and a moment later Helen and her brother came in. As Percy's case was merely one of detention, or for some other obscurer reason, known only to those who took their orders from McCarthy, the three were left alone to their own devices.

At the sight of Helen's trim tailor-clad figure Percy's expression brightened to what, in his case, might almost be called animation. He swept aside the accumulation of papers, and made room for both. After the first greetings and exclamations, Helen demanded to know particulars and prospects.

"All right, I'll tell you," agreed Darrow.

The Sign at Six

"I'm thought out; and I want to hear it myself."

Jack looked about him uneasily.

"Is it wise to talk here?" he asked. "I don't doubt they have arrangements for overhearing anything that is said."

"I don't think they care what we say," observed Darrow. "They are merely detaining me on some excuse or another that I haven't even taken the trouble to inquire about."

"That must astonish them some," said Jack.

"And if they do overhear, I don't much care. Now," said he, turning to Helen, "we have here three strange happenings comprising two phenomena—the cutting off of the electricity, first in the Atlas Building, second in the city at large; and the cutting off of sound in the Atlas. Although we are, of course, not justified in generalizing from one instance, what would you think by analogy would be the next thing to expect?"

The Sign at Six

"That sound would be cut off in the city," said Helen; "but Jack has already delivered me your warning or advice," she added.

"Precisely. Now as to theories of the ultimate cause. Naturally this must have been brought about either by nature or by man. If by nature, it is exceedingly localized, not to say directed. If by man, he must have in some way acquired unprecedented powers over the phenomena of electricity and sound. These he can evidently, at will, either focus, as on the Atlas Building, or diffuse, as over the city. For the moment we will adopt the latter hypothesis."

"That it is a man in possession of extraordinary powers," said Helen, leaning forward in her interest. "Go on."

"We have, completed, only the phenomena of electricity," continued Darrow; "the phenomena of sound remain to be completed. We observe as to that (a)"—he folded back his

The Sign at Six

forefinger—"the Atlas manifestation lasted about nine and a half hours; and (b)"—he folded his middle finger—"the city manifestation was a little less than two hours."

"Yes," cried Jack, "but then this second—"

"One minute," interrupted Darrow; "let me finish. Now, let us place ourselves in the position of a man possessed of a new toy, or a new power which he has never tried out! What would he do?"

"Try it out," said Jack.

"Certainly; try it out to the limit, to see just what it could do in different circumstances. Now, take the lapses of time I have mentioned, and assume, for the sake of argument, that these powers are limited."

"Just how do you mean—limited?" asked Helen.

"I mean exhaustible, like a watering-pot. You can water just so much, and then you have to go back and fill up again. In that case, we

The Sign at Six

can suppose this man's stream will last nine hours and a half when he dribbles it down on one spot, like the Atlas Building; but it will empty itself in about two hours when he turns her upside down over a whole city. There remains only the length of time necessary to refill the water-pot to round out our hypothesis. That is something more than nine hours and something less than fifteen."

"How do you get those figures?" demanded Jack.

"The Unknown is anxious, after the Atlas success, to try out his discovery on the larger scale. He will naturally do so at the first opportunity after his water-pot is refilled. But he wishes to do so at the first effective opportunity. What is the most effective moment? The rush hours. What are the rush hours? From eight to ten, and at six. Since he did not pull off his show in the morning, we are fairly justified in concluding, tentatively, that the

The Sign at Six

water-pot was not full by then, and, as the Atlas phenomena subsided at three of the morning before, the inference is obvious."

"But isn't the most effective time at night, anyway, on account of the lights?" asked Jack.

"Good boy!" approved Darrow. "He might have waited for that. But the city-wide phenomena ceased at eight the night before; and the Atlas sound phenomena did not occur until ten the next morning—fourteen hours. Now, the most effective time to scare McCarthy was any time after nine. McCarthy arrives as the clock strikes."

Jack shook his head.

"Oh, it's not proof; it's idle hypothesis," admited Darrow. "We shall have to test it. But let's go on with it, anyway, and see how it works out."

"What's McCarthy got to do with it?" demanded Helen.

"That's so, you aren't in touch there." Dar-

85

The Sign at Six

row sketched briefly the situation as it affected the boss. Helen's eyes were shining with interest.

"Now," continued Darrow, "having tried out his new power to the limit, our friend would begin to use it only as he needed it. There is now no reason to empty the water-pot entirely. All he wanted to do this morning was to scare McCarthy, and impress the public. He did that in thirty-eight minutes. On the basis of fourteen hours to fill the water-pot, it is evident that he would be rehabilitated, ready for business, in an hour. Therefore, all he is waiting for now is the most effective moment to try out his city-wide experiment of silence. I imagine that will be about six."

"Sounds reasonable," admitted Jack.

"Reasonable! It's certain!" cried Helen.

Darrow smiled. "No, only a wild hypothesis."

"It'll scare people to death," observed Jack.

The Sign at Six

"They're scared already; and they're somewhat prepared by the performance this morning. Besides, I don't see yet that human agency is suspected."

"Don't you think you'd better warn people what is going to happen, and tell them there's nothing to be frightened of?" pleaded Helen.

"No," said Darrow, "I do not. It would confuse the phenomena, and they must be unconfused in order that I can either prove or disprove my hypothesis. If this lasts about two hours, the fact will go far to prove me right. If the next manifestation comes at about ten the next morning, we shall have established a periodicity, at least. But if the man realizes that his existence is suspected, he will purposely vary in order to mix me up."

"The next manifestation!" cried Helen. "Then you think they will continue—"

"Why not," smiled Darrow, "until he has scared McCarthy out?"

The Sign at Six

"Which will it be next time, do you think?"

"Whatever happens, don't be frightened," said Darrow enigmatically.

"It seems to me there is something absurd about all this," said Helen. "A man with such a discovery, such powers, using them in such a manner, for such a petty purpose!"

"He is, of course, crazy," Darrow said quietly; "the methodical logical lunatic—the most dangerous sort."

"What is it he has discovered?" asked Jack.

"I do not know, yet."

"But you suspect?"

Darrow nodded, but would not explain.

"What will be the outcome?"

"I am going to cut loose from science and guess wildly," said Darrow, after a moment. "To-morrow morning, somewhere about ten, McCarthy will disappear."

"You said that before!" cried Jack.

"Well, I say it again," drawled Darrow.

CHAPTER IX

THE GREAT SILENCE

PERCY DARROW sat quite calmly, though a little hungrily, through the first of the two hours of the Great Silence. As it fell, he looked at his watch; then went on reading. Strangely terrified faces flitted by the open door of his little room. About seven o'clock Darrow, struck by a sudden idea, arose, walked down the corridor outside, and quite deliberately set to work to force the light door. As has been intimated, either by direct order of McCarthy or because of some vagueness of the orders, the young man had been confined, not in the jail proper, but in one of the living apartments of the wing.

The Sign at Six

Few realize how important a rôle sound plays in what might be called the defensives of our every-day life. Sight is important, to be sure, but it is more often corroborative than not; it is more often used to identify the source of the alarm that has been communicated through other channels. When we are told of the hero—or the villain—that he stood "with every sense alert", our mental picture, in spite of the phrasing, is that of a man listening intently for the first intimations of what may threaten.

So it is in prison. The warders can, of necessity, remain within actual view of but a few of the prisoners a small proportion of the time. But through those massive and silent corridors sound stands watch-dog for them. The minute scratch of a file, the vibrations attendant on the most cautious attempts against the stone structure, the most muffled footfall reports to the jailer that mischief is afoot. In-

The Sign at Six

stantly he is on the spot to corroborate by his other faculties the warnings of the watch-dog of the senses.

Now the watch-dog was asleep. Percy Darrow reflected that, were it not for the terror of these unexplainable hours, the prisoners within or their friends without could assail their confines boldly and formidably, even with dynamite, and none would be the wiser if only none happened to be within actual visual range of the operations. He himself quite coolly used the iron side piece to his bed as a battering-ram to break the locks of the door. Then he walked down the long corridor and out through the police station, bowing politely to the bewildered officers. The latter did not attempt to stop him.

The people in the streets were, for the most part, either standing stock-still, or moving slowly forward in a groping sort of fashion. Darrow, for the second time, noticed how anal-

The Sign at Six

ogous to the deprivation of sight was the total deprivation of hearing and feeling vibration.

Traffic was at a standstill. People's faces were bewildered, for the most part; though here and there one showed contorted with the hysteria of fright, or exalted with some other, probably religious, emotion. The same impression of ghostliness came to Darrow here as in the Atlas Building. Visual causes were not producing their wonted aural effect.

On the street corner a peanut vender's little whistle sent aloft bravely its jet of steam; the bells on a ragpicker's cart swung merrily back and forth on their strap; a big truck, whose driver was either undaunted or drunk, banged and clattered and rattled over the rough cobbles of a side street—but no sound came from any one of them.

This complete severance of one cause and effect was sufficient to discredit all natural laws. No other cause and effect was certain.

The Sign at Six

Everywhere people were touching things to see if they were solid, or wet, or soft, or hard, as the case might be. Even Darrow felt, absurdly enough, that it would not be greatly serious to jump off the top of any building into the street.

Darrow swung confidently enough down the street. He was the only person, with the exception of the drunken truck driver, who moved forward at a natural and easy gait. The effect was startling. Darrow seemed to be the only real human being of the lot. All the rest were phantasmagoric.

But as he proceeded down-town the spell was beginning to break. People were communicating with one another by means of pencil and paper. Darrow was amused, on crossing the park, to see against the lighted windows on Newspaper Row the silhouetted forms of activity. Evidently, the newspaper men were already at work on this fresh story.

Near the corner of the park Darrow saw

The Sign at Six

standing a policeman of his varied acquaintance. The scientist walked up to this man, who was standing in the typical vacant uncertainty, smiled agreeably, clapped him on the back, and shook his hand. The patrolman grasped Darrow's hand, but the look of groping uncertainty deepened on his face.

Darrow slipped his note-book from his pocket, and scribbled a few lines, which he showed to the officer. The latter read, inwardly digested for a moment, and smiled.

"Keep your hair on," ran Darrow's screed. "This will pass in a few minutes, and it won't hurt you, anyway. Don't look like all these other dubs."

He stood there companionably by the patrolman. They looked about them. All at once, with this touch of normal, unafraid, human companionship, the weird horror of the situation fell away. Darrow and his companion were seeing humanity disjointed from its ac-

The Sign at Six

customed habit, as one looks on a stage full of men hypnotized into belief of an absurdity.

Where the blotting out of electricity had been tragic, this, as soon as its utter harmlessness was realized, became comic. All about through the park men were meeting the situation according to the limited ideas developed by a crustacean life of absolute dependence on the shell of artificial environment. A considerable number of all sorts had fallen on their knees and were praying. One fat man in evening dress, with a silk hat and a large diamond stud showing between the lapels of a fur-lined coat, was particularly fervent. By force of habit Darrow remarked on this individual.

"I'll bet he hasn't been to church since he was a kid," he observed, of course inaudibly.

The policeman caught the direction of his look, however, and grinned with understanding.

Some stood frozen to one spot, their faces

95

The Sign at Six

agonized, as a man would stand still were the earth likely to yawn anywhere. Darrow would have liked to reassure these, for their eyes expressed a frantic terror. One red-faced individual with white side-whiskers, looking exactly like the comic-paper caricatures of the trusts, had evidently refused to accept any arbitrary dictates of natural forces. Probably he had never accepted any dictates of any kind. He was going from one taxicab to another, trying to command a driver to take him somewhere, talking vehemently and authoritatively, his face getting more and more purple with anger. The taxicab drivers merely stared at him stupidly.

"That old boy's kept his nerve," Darrow remarked, of course inaudibly, to his companion. "But he'll die of apoplexy if he doesn't watch out."

Again the policeman caught the direction of Darrow's glance, and grinned in understand-

The Sign at Six

ing. He reached his huge gloved hand for the young man's pencil and paper, on which he wrote the name of a man high in railroad circles, and grinned again with evident relish.

At this moment an entirely self-possessed young man swung across the street. He surveyed the two men sharply a moment, then approached, producing a sheaf of yellow paper as he did so.

"Professor Darrow?" he wrote.

Darrow nodded.

The young man pointed to himself, then to the Despatch Building.

"Cause?" he wrote, and waved his hand.

Darrow shook his head.

"Dangerous?"

Darrow shook his head again.

The reporter was about to add another question, when Darrow reached for the paper. It was thrust eagerly into his hand. Darrow consulted his watch.

The Sign at Six

"If," he wrote, "you will wait here four minutes, I'll give you an interview."

The reporter read this, and nodded.

"You're on!" he added to the written dialogue. Then he produced a cigarette, lighted it, and joined the other two men in their amused survey of the public's performances.

During the four minutes that ensued Darrow examined the reporter speculatively. Finally his eye lighted up with recollection.

CHAPTER X

THE LIFTING OF THE SPELL

THE spell lifted. The city broke into a roar. People sprang into rapid and violent motion, as though released from a physical lethargy.

"All over?" asked the reporter. He asked it in a loud shout.

"All over," replied Darrow. "You don't need to yell. I'm not deaf."

The reporter grinned.

"I guess that's what everybody else in town is doing," he surmised.

Certainly this remark was justified by the sample in the square. Every man was shouting at his neighbor to the lung-straining limit

99

of his ability. Three exhorters, their eyes ablaze with fanaticism, began to thunder forth dire warnings of the wrath to come—and gained a hearing. Men rushed to and fro aimlessly. The gentleman with the side-whiskers, who looked like the caricatures of the trusts, having at last succeeded in making his imperial wishes known, clambered into a taxicab, and sat back, apparently unimpressed. After a moment the driver recovered sufficiently to fall into the habit of obedience, and so drove away.

While the three men watched, a burly individual with a red face came hurtling directly at them. If they had not dodged hastily to one side, they would have suffered a collision.

"The end of the world is at hand!" this man was shrieking. "Repent! Repent!"

"That's Larry Mulcahey," remarked the reporter, with a grin. "He keeps bar."

"I'm hungry," observed Darrow. "Haven't eaten since noon."

The Sign at Six

"Free lunch," suggested the reporter practically. "You won't be able to get any service anywhere. How about that interview? Got anything to say?"

"You're the busy little bee to-night," said Darrow. "But I'll tell you what I'll do. I'll give you a tip. Be at the Atlas Building at not later than nine to-morrow morning, and stay at least until ten. If you can fix it, be on the tenth floor. Hunt up the United Wireless man and make him talk. Then come to me."

"That's afternoon paper stuff—unless it's exclusive," said the reporter instantly.

"If you'll obey my orders the most important part of it will be exclusive," said Darrow.

The reporter eyed him keenly.

"Why?" he asked.

"You're Hallowell, aren't you? I thought I wasn't mistaken. I saw you at work on that Duane Street murder case. Your work was good. Besides, I like the *Despatch*—and the

The Sign at Six

afternoon papers are too soon for what I want."

"Last reason accepted. Others received and placed on file."

"All right," agreed Darrow. "Have it your own way—only obey orders." He entered the door of the bar and advanced on the lunch counter.

CHAPTER XI

AT nine o'clock the following morning five men grouped in McCarthy's office, talking earnestly. Darrow and Jack Warford had been the first to arrive. McCarthy did not seem surprised to see them; nor did he greet them with belligerence.

"Well?" he demanded.

"Well?" repeated Darrow, sinking gracefully to one corner of the table. "You're an old fool, McCarthy. What good did you think it would do you to arrest me?"

"I intended to sweat you," confessed the boss frankly, "but I was too busy."

"Sweat me, eh?" demanded Darrow, with

103

The Sign at Six

some amusement. "So you decided not to, did you—hence the lack of enthusiasm on the part of the police in effecting my recapture. You didn't imagine I caused all this, did you?"

"I don't know," growled McCarthy. "But if you, or the other fellow, or whoever or whatever it is, think you can bluff me out, you or he or it's left! That's all!"

"So you've been getting more wireless, have you?" surmised Darrow.

McCarthy cast a surly glance toward Jack, whom previously he had ignored.

"Yes," he admitted grudgingly.

Darrow held out his hand. After a moment's hesitation McCarthy thrust forward a single yellow paper, and Darrow read aloud in spite of the boss' warning gesture:

"McCarthy: The sign has been sent you and sent your people. You are stubborn, but it shall not avail you. You must go; and within twenty-four hours. It will not avail

The Sign at Six

you unless you go. The *Celtic* leaves to-morrow at noon. You must go on that ship. I shall know whether or not you obey me. Once more I shall warn you; one more sign shall I send. Then I shall strike!"

"He's getting garrulous," remarked Darrow reflectively; "but he's relieved my mind. You'd better go."

"Go!" cried McCarthy, half starting to his feet. "Not on your life!"

Darrow surveyed him calmly.

"You're getting rattled," said he, "and it doesn't pay you particularly to try to bluff me. A jack-rabbit of average firmness could stampede you in your present state of mind."

"You think so?" sneered McCarthy.

"I know so. And you're quite right. If you attempt the game too long, he'll destroy you."

"How?" demanded McCarthy.

"Take my word for it, *he can do it!*" replied Darrow.

The Sign at Six

McCarthy ruminated, drumming his thick fingers on the desk.

"Find him," said he, at last.

"I intend to," replied Darrow.

"That'll be all right about your friend's job," conceded McCarthy, with a nod toward Jack.

"I fancy you won't have anything to do with it," returned Darrow pleasantly.

At this moment the door opened and Hallowell entered. He nodded to Darrow, and greeted McCarthy.

"Nothing for you," growled the latter.

Darrow glanced at his watch.

"He will have in about five minutes," said he to the reporter.

The fifth member of the party now entered in the person of Simmons, the United Wireless operator. On seeing the number gathered in McCarthy's office he came to a halt.

Darrow immediately detached himself from the group and approached this man.

The Sign at Six

"Anything new?" he inquired in a low voice.

Simmons glanced toward McCarthy.

"New about what?" he demanded stolidly.

"Any more messages from our mysterious friend out in the ether to our equally mysterious friend at the desk?"

"I don't know what you mean."

Darrow surveyed him reflectively.

"This is a pretty big story," he said at last, "and affects a lot of people. If you really haven't leaked—well, he"—with a jerk of his head toward McCarthy—"must bribe high, or have a strangle hold on you for fair."

He looked around to see the boss' eye fixed intently on him, smiled pleasantly, and moved to one side. Simmons stepped forward, handed McCarthy a paper, and went out. The boss read the message slowly, and turned a little pale. After a moment or so he surreptitiously drew out his watch. Percy Darrow smiled. He, too, held his watch in his hand.

The Sign at Six

"Thirty seconds more—about," he remarked pleasantly. The boss looked up startled. The last thing he saw was the faintly smiling, triumphant face of the young scientist. Then absolute blackness fell on him.

For several seconds astonishment held the inmates of the room chained to their places; and for that space of time no sound broke the deathly stillness. Then Percy Darrow spoke, in his natural voice.

"Well, Jack," he remarked, "it worked out, to a second, almost. Now I'm certain."

As though this breaking of the silence had released a force hitherto held in repression, the room filled with tumult and clamor, with crashing, banging and scurrying of heavy bodies. A final concussion shook the air, and then, again abruptly, silence fell.

"Say!" Hallowell's voice spoke up, a trifle uncertainly. "I'll stand for most any kind of a dark séance, but this particular spook business is getting on my nerves. Are you there, Dar-row?"

"Yes, I'm here," answered the scientist.

"Well, can you explain *that* phenomenon?"

"That," drawled Darrow, a slight note of laughter in his voice, "was that extraordinary upheaval of natural forces known as Brother McCarthy going away from here—hastily."

Jack chuckled.

"He hit me on the way out," remarked that young man. "I'll testify he was a solid spook."

The reporter was methodically striking match after match, but without result. After a moment the acrid smell of burning woolen rose in the air.

"Are you dropping those matches?" asked Darrow.

"Sure; they're no good."

"Well, they're good enough to burn holes in McCarthy's rugs. Stamp around a little to put them out; and quit it."

The Sign at Six

"What next; and how long?" asked Jack. "What is it? Have we gone blind, or is it a total eclipse, or what?"

"I don't know how long," came back Darrow's voice calmly. "Next we will get out of the building. I want to make some observations. Get hold of my hand; we'll have to grope our way out."

"If we could only get a light," muttered Hallowell.

"You can't," stated Darrow.

They felt their way down the ten flights of stairs like blind men. A few inmates of the building they jostled, or passed, or picked up on the way.

"This settles it," one remarked profanely. "My lease quits. They can sue and be damned. I decline to have anything more to do with any freak-lined skyscraper of this description.'"

In the lower corridors Darrow halted them.

"Here's another thing," said he: "if I'm

The Sign at Six

right, we should run out of this just eleven feet beyond the last elevator cage."

He felt his way along the grill, made four paces forward, and uttered a little cry of satisfaction. The two men followed him blindly. As though stepping from one room to another they emerged into glaring daylight!

Both involuntarily looked back. The darkness hung there like a curtain, just inside the outer walls of the building. Already a crowd had gathered to observe this new and strange phenomenon of the now celebrated Atlas Building. It was a curious and a facetious crowd, but not awestricken, as it had been at the first manifestations of this freakish upset of natural forces.

A man observing the flight of an aeroplane for the first time loses his sense of strangeness inside of a few minutes; and yet flying has been since the days of Icarus considered one of the impossible achievements. So the general

III

The Sign at Six

public of Manhattan were becoming accustomed to reversals of form in the affairs of the physical world. The frivolous majority, having discovered nothing to be apprehended from the phenomena save a few hours' helplessness of a sort, and much to be gained through the savor of novelty, were inclined to an amused or irritated attitude, depending on the extent to which its occupations were interfered with. The minority took to religious meetings and interpretations.

Darrow's exit, and that of his companions, was greeted uproariously.

" 'Please go 'way an' let me sleep!' " sang one, at the blinking men.

"Here's another!" shrilled a gamin. "Get up! The porter wants to make up your berth!"

Several of the crowd, pending the usual arrival of the police to clear the corridor, had ventured through the wide portals, and were

The Sign at Six

experimenting with this strange palpable quality of darkness. One or two popped inside the curtain, but emerged quickly, looking a little scared.

A bright youth made the discovery that if one lighted a match and stepped within the blackness, the match was immediately extinguished, but that upon emerging into daylight the flame came up again. Some one happened along with a plumber's gasoline torch. Immediately this was lighted and the experiment repeated. The bearer of the torch, astonished at the instant extinguishment of the flame, felt with his hand to see what could be the matter. Instantly he uttered a yelp of pain, and leaped outside, displaying a badly burned palm.

"There wasn't no flame; I swear it!" he explained excitedly, "but she burned, just the same!" He rushed about from one to another, displaying his injured palm to whoever would look.

The Sign at Six

Darrow paid little attention to this gathering crowd. First of all, he scanned a paper he held in his hand; then plunged back again into the blackness.

Jack Warford and Hallowell, left together, hesitated uncertainly.

"He'll be back," the reporter decided finally, "and he's the man to tie to."

While waiting, he proceeded to pick up what information he could from the bystanders. It seemed that the first intimation of anything wrong was followed very shortly by the emergence of McCarthy, disheveled, hatless, staring, gasping. The boss had stumbled into the street, hesitated, then started south on a run. Before any one could stop him, he had turned a corner and disappeared. The excitement at the Atlas Building had distracted attention from him. Nobody wondered at his getting rattled and running away. The few tenants remaining in the building had stumbled forth,

The Sign at Six

vowing never to return to such a—assorted adjectives—building. That was all there seemed to be to say.

In the meantime the crowd had increased from a few hundred to thousands. Police appeared. The corridors were cleared of all but a few. Among these were Hallowell and Jack Warford; the former as a reporter, the latter as the reporter's companion. Doctor Knox and Professor Eldridge arrived shortly. After a time Darrow reappeared, sauntering quite calmly from the pall of darkness, as though emerging from behind a velvet curtain.

CHAPTER XII.

THE UNKNOWN

IT will now become necessary to glance in passing at the personal characteristics of Professor Eldridge. This man was in about his fortieth year, tall, spare, keenly intellectual in countenance, cold, possessed of an absolute reliance on the powers of science, beyond which his mental processes did not stray. His manner was distinguished by a stiff unbending formality; his expression by a glacial coldness of steel-gray eyes and a straight-line compression of thin lips; his dress by a precise and unvarying formalism, and his speech by a curious polysyllabic stiffness.

This latter idiosyncrasy would, in another,

The Sign at Six

have seemed either priggish or facetiously intended. With Professor Eldridge it was merely a natural method of speech. Thus, arriving once at the stroke of the dinner hour, he replied to compliments on his punctuality by remarking:

"I have always considered punctuality a virtue when one is invited to partake of gratuitous nourishment."

Withal, his scientific attainments were not only undoubted, but so considerable as to have won for him against many odds the reputation of a great scientist. His specialty, if such it might be called, was scientific diagnosis. The exactness of scientific laws was so admirably duplicated by the exactitudes of his mind that he seemed able, by a bloodless and mechanical sympathy, to penetrate to the most obscure causes of the strangest events. It might be added that practically his only social ties were those with the Warfords, and that the only

The Sign at Six

woman with whom he ever entered into conversation was Helen.

At sight of him Percy Darrow's lounging
gait became accentuated to exaggeration.

"Hello, Prof!" he drawled. "On the job, I
see. Good morning, Doctor," he greeted Knox.
"What do you make of it?"

"I make of it that the Atlas Building will
shortly be without tenants," replied the doctor;
"me, for one."

Eldridge surveyed Darrow coldly through
the glittering toric lenses of his glasses.

"The cause of these extraordinary phenomena is self-evident," he stated.

"You mean their nature, not their cause,"
replied Darrow. "In nature, they refer back to
the interference with etheric and molecular
vibrations. That," he added, "is a fact that
every boy in the grammar-school physics class
has figured out for himself. The cause is a
different matter."

The Sign at Six

"I stand corrected," said Eldridge. "Such lapses in accuracy of statement are not usual with me, but may be considered as concomitant with unusual circumstances."

"Right-o!" agreed Darrow cheerfully. "Well, what about the causes?"

"That I will determine when I am satisfied that all the elements of the problem are in my hands."

"Right-o!" repeated Darrow. "Well, I'll bet you a new hat I'll land the cause before you do. Be a sport!"

"I never indulge in wagers," replied Eldridge.

"Well," said Darrow to Jack and Hallowell, "come on!"

Without waiting to see if he was followed, the young man again plunged into the black and clinging darkness.

"Get hold of my coat," his voice came to the others. "We're going to climb."

119

The Sign at Six

Accordingly they climbed, in silence, up many flights of stairs, through the cloying darkness. At last Darrow halted, turned sharp to the left, fumbled for a door, and entered a room.

"Simmons?" he said.

"Here!" came a voice.

"I thought you'd be on the job," said Darrow, with satisfaction. "How's your instrument? Going, eh? We are in the wireless offices," he told the others. "Sit down, if you can find chairs. We'll wait until the sun is shining brightly, love, before we really try to get down to business. In the meantime—"

"In the meantime—" repeated both Jack and Hallowell, in a breath. "Go on, my son," conceded the latter. "I bet we have the same idea."

"Well, I was going to say that I'm not in the grammar-school physics class, and I want to know what you meant by your remark to Eldridge," said Jack.

The Sign at Six

"That's my trouble," said Hallowell.

"It's simple enough," began Darrow. "We have had, first, a failure of all electricity; second, a failure of all sound; third, a failure of all light. The logical mind would therefore examine these things to see what they have in common. The answer simply jumps at you: *Vibration*. Electricity and light are vibrations in ether; sound is vibration in air or some solid. Therefore, whatever could absolutely stop vibration would necessarily stop electricity, light and sound."

"But," objected Jack, "if vibration were absolutely stopped, why wouldn't they all three be blotted out at once?"

"Because," explained Darrow, "the vibrations making these three phenomena are different in character. Sound is made by horizontal waves, for example, while electricity and light are made by transverse waves. Furthermore, the waves producing electricity and light

121

differ in length. Now, it is conceivable that a condition which would interfere with horizontal waves would not interfere with transverse waves; or that a condition which would absolutely deaden waves two hundred and seventy ten-millionths of an inch long would have absolutely no effect on those one hundred and fifty-five ten-millionths of an inch long. Am I clear?"

"Sure!" came the voices of his audience.

"That much Eldridge and any other man trained in elementary science already knows. It is no secret."

"It hasn't been published," observed Hallowell grimly.

"Well, go to it! The task of the independent investigator, of which we are some, is now to discover, first, what are those conditions, and, second, what causes them. With the exception of Mr. Hallowell, we all know what this guiding power is."

The Sign at Six

"Don't get it," growled Simmons.

"Now, look here, Simmons, you are very loyal to McCarthy, for whatever reason, but your loyalty is misplaced. For one thing, your man has disappeared, and will not return. That last message scared him out. For another thing, we're going to need you in our campaign, the worst way."

"I'm from Copenhagen; you got to show me," said Simmons.

Darrow laughed softly.

"We'll show you, all right," said he. He sketched briefly for Hallowell's benefit the reasoning already followed out, and which it is therefore unnecessary to repeat here. "So now," he concluded, "we will consider this hypothesis: that these phenomena are caused by one man in control of a force capable of deadening vibrations in ether and solids within certain definite limits."

"Why do you limit it?" cried Hallowell.

The Sign at Six

"Because we have had but one manifestation at a time. If this Unknown were out really to frighten—which seems to be his intention—it would be much more effective to visit us with absolute darkness and absolute silence combined. That would be really terrifying. He has not done so. Therefore, I conclude that his power is limited in applicability."

"Isn't that a little doubtful?" spoke up Jack.

"Of course," said Darrow cheerfully. "That's where we're going to win out on this sporting proposition with our dear Brother Eldridge. He won't accept any hypothesis unless it is absolutely copper-riveted. We will."

"I think you underestimate Eldridge," spoke up Hallowell. "He's the only original think-tank in a village of horse troughs."

"I don't underestimate him one bit," countered Darrow; "but we have a head start on him with our reasoning; that's all. He's absolutely sure to come to the conclusions I have

124

The Sign at Six

just detailed, only he'll get there a little more slowly. That's why I want you in on this thing, Hallowell."

"How's that?"

"We'll publish everything up to date and cut the ground from under him."

"What's your special grouch on Eldridge, anyway?" asked Jack.

"I like to worry him," replied Percy Darrow non-committally.

At this moment the darkness disappeared as though some one had turned a switch. The reporter, the operator and the scientist's young assistant moved involuntarily as though dodging, and blinked. Darrow shaded his eyes with one hand and proceeded as though nothing had happened.

"Here are the exclusive points of your story," he said to Hallowell, handing him a sheaf of yellow wireless forms. "I got them in McCarthy's office. They are messages from

The Sign at Six

the unknown wielder of the mysterious power to his enemy, the political boss. There will be plenty who will conclude these messages to be the result of fanaticism, after the fact; that is to say, they will conclude some wireless amateur has taken advantage of natural phenomena and, by claiming himself the author of them, has attempted to use them against his enemy. Of course, the answer to that is that if the Unknown—let's call him Monsieur X—did not cause these strange things, he at least knew enough about them to predict them accurately."

"You just leave that to me," hummed Hallowell under his breath. The reporter had been glancing over the wireless forms, and his eyes were shining with delight.

"Here is the last one," said Darrow, producing a crumpled yellow paper from his pocket. "I went back after it."

"McCarthy: My patience is at an end. Your last warning will be sent you at nine

The Sign at Six

thirty this morning. If you do not sail on the *Celtic* at noon I shall strike. You are of a stubborn and a stiff-necked generation, but I am your lord and master, and my wrath shall be visited on you. Begone, or you shall die the death."

"That bluffed him out," said Darrow, "and I don't blame him. Now, Simmons," said he, turning to the operator, who had sat in utter silence, "how about it? Are you with us, or against us?"

"How do you mean?" demanded Simmons.

"This," said Darrow sharply. "The time has passed for concealment. Every message through the ether must now reach the public. We must send messages back. The case is out of private hands; it has become important to the people. Will you agree on your honor faithfully to transmit?" He leaned forward, his indolent frame startlingly tense. "Are you afraid of McCarthy?"

The Sign at Six

"He's been good to me—it's a family matter," muttered the operator.

"Well—" Darrow arose, crossed to the operator, and whispered to him for a moment. "You see the seriousness—you are an intelligent man."

The operator turned pale.

"I hadn't thought of that," he muttered. "I hadn't thought of that. Of course I'm with you."

"I thought you would be," drawled Percy Darrow slowly. "If you hadn't decided to be, I'd have had another man put in your place. Hadn't thought of that, either, had you?"

"No, sir," replied Simmons.

"Well, I prefer you. It's no job for a quitter, and I believe you'll stick."

"I'll stick," repeated Simmons.

"Well, to work," said Darrow, lighting the cigarette he had been playing with. "Send this out, and see if you can reach Monsieur X.

The Sign at Six

" '*M*,' " he dictated slowly. " 'Do you get this?' Repeat that until you get a reply."

Without comment the operator turned to his key. The long ripping crashes of the wireless sender followed the movements of his fingers.

"I get his '*I—I*,' " he said, after a moment. "It's almighty faint."

"Good!" said Darrow. "Give him this:

" 'McCarthy has disappeared. Can no longer reach him with your messages.' "

"He merely answers '*I—I*,' " observed the operator.

"By the way," asked Darrow, "what is your shift, anyhow? Weren't you on at night when this thing began?"

"I'm still on at night; but Mr. McCarthy sent me a message, and asked me to stay on all this morning as a personal favor to him."

"I see. Then you're still on at night?"

"Yes, sir."

"Well, tell Monsieur X that fact, put yourself at his disposal, and tell him he'd better get all his messages to you rather than to the other operators here."

"All right."

"There's your story," said Darrow to Hallowell; "it's in those messages. The scientific aspect will probably be done by somebody for the evening papers. You better concentrate on Monsieur X's connection with McCarthy."

"Say, my friend," said Hallowell earnestly, "do you think I'm a reporter for the *Scientific American* or a newspaper?"

All three rose. The operator was busy crashing away at his Leyden jars.

"What next?" asked Jack.

"That depends on two things."

"Whether or not McCarthy takes the *Celtic*," interposed Hallowell quickly.

"And whether Monsieur X will be satisfied with his mere disappearance, if he does not take the *Celtic*," supplemented Darrow. "In

The Sign at Six

any case, we've got to find him. He's unbalanced; he possesses an immense and disconcerting and a dangerous power; he is becoming possessed of a *manie des grandeurs*. You remember the phrasing of his last message? 'I am your lord and master, and my wrath shall be visited on you. Begone!' That is the language of exaltation. Exaltation is not far short of irresponsible raving."

"What possible clue—" began Jack Warford blankly.

"When a man is somewhere out in the ether there is no clue," replied Darrow.

"Then how on earth can you hope to find him?"

"By the exercise of pure reason," said Darrow calmly.

CHAPTER XIII

DARROW'S CHALLENGE

WITH a final warning to Simmons as to the dissemination of any information without consulting him, Darrow left the room. Hallowell listened to this advice with unmixed satisfaction; the afternoon papers would not be able to get at his source of information. The reporter felt a slight wonder as to how Darrow had managed his ascendency over the operator. An inquiry as to that met with a shake of the head.

"I may have to ask your help in that later," was his only reply.

At the corner, after pushing through a curious crowd, the men separated. Hallowell

132

The Sign at Six

started for the wharf; Jack Warford for home
—at Darrow's request. The scientist returned
to his own apartments, where he locked himself in and sat for five hours cross-legged on a
divan, staring straight ahead of him, doing
nothing. At the end of that time he cautiously
stretched his legs, sighed, rose, and looked into
the mirror.

"I guess you're hungry," he remarked to the
image therein.

It was now near mid-afternoon. Percy
Darrow wandered out, ate a leisurely meal at
the nearest restaurant, and sauntered up the
avenue. He paused at a news stand to buy an
afternoon paper, glanced at the head-lines and a
portion of the text, and smiled sweetly to himself. Then he betook himself by means of a
bus to the Warford residence.

Helen was at home, and in the library. With
her was Professor Eldridge. The men greeted
each other formally. After a moment of gen-

eral conversation Darrow produced the newspaper.

"I see you have your theories in print," he
drawled. "Very interesting. I didn't know
you'd undertaken grammar-school physics instruction."

"I know I'm going to be grateful for any
sort of instruction—from anybody," interposed
Helen. "I'm all in the dark."

"Like the Atlas Building," Darrow smiled
at her. "Well, here's a very good exposition
in words of one syllable. I'll leave you the
paper. Professor, what have you concluded as
to the causes?"

"They are yet to be determined."

"Pardon me," drawled Darrow, "they have
been determined—or at least their controlling
power."

"In what way, may I ask?" inquired Professor Eldridge formally.

"Very simply. By the exercise of a little

The Sign at Six

reason. I am going to tell you, because I want you to start fairly with me; and because you'll know all about it in the morning, anyway."

"Your idea—the one you told us yesterday—is to be published?" cried Helen, leaning forward with interest.

"The basis of it will be," replied Darrow. "Now"—he turned to Eldridge—"listen carefully; I'm not going to indulge in many explanations. Malachi McCarthy, political boss of this city, has made a personal enemy of a half-crazed or at least unbalanced man, who has in some way gained a limited power over etheric and other vibrations. This power Monsieur X, as I call him—the Unknown—has employed in fantastic manifestations designed solely for the purpose of frightening his enemy into leaving this country."

Eldridge was listening with the keenest attention, his cold gray eyes glittering frostily behind their toric lenses.

The Sign at Six

"You support your major hypothesis, I suppose?" he demand calmly.

"By wireless messages sent from Monsieur X to McCarthy, in which he predicts or appoints in advance the exact hour at which these manifestations take place."

"In advance, I understand you to say?"

"Precisely."

"The proof is as conclusive for merely prophetic ability as for power over the phenomena."

"In formal logic; not in common sense."

Eldridge reflected a moment further, removing his glasses, with the edge of which he tapped methodically the palm of his left hand. Helen had sunk back into the depths of her armchair, and was watching with immobile countenance but vividly interested eyes the progress of the duel.

"Granting for the moment your major hypothesis," Eldridge stated at last, "I follow your

The Sign at Six

other essential statements. The man is unbalanced because he chooses such a method of accomplishing a simple end."

"Quite so."

"His power is limited because it has been applied to but one manifestation of etheric vibration at a time; and each manifestation has had a defined duration."

Darrow bowed. "You are the only original think-tank," he quoted Hallowell's earlier remark.

"You are most kind to place me in possession of these additional facts," said Eldridge, resuming his glasses, "for naturally my conclusions, based on incomplete premises, could hardly be considered more than tentative. The happy accident of an acquaintance with the existence of these wireless messages and this personal enmity gave you a manifest but artificial advantage in the construction of your hypothesis."

The Sign at Six

"Did I not see you in the corridor of the Atlas Building the day of the first electrical failure?" asked Darrow.

"Certainly."

"Then you had just as much to go on as I did," drawled Darrow, half closing his eyes. The long dark lashes fell across his cheek, investing him in his most harmless and effeminate look.

"I fail to—"

"Yes, you fail, all right," interrupted Darrow. "You had all the strings in your hands, but you were a mile behind me in the solution of this mystery. I'll tell you why: it was for the same reason that you're going to fail a second time, now that once again I've put all the strings in your hands."

"I must confess I fail to gather your meaning," said Professor Eldridge coldly.

"It was for the same reason that always until his death you were inferior to dear old

138

The Sign at Six

Doctor Schermerhorn as a scientist. You are an almost perfect thinking machine."

Darrow quite deliberately lighted a cigarette, flipped the match into the grate, and leaned back luxuriously. Professor Eldridge sat bolt upright, waiting. Helen Warford watched them both.

"You have no humanity; you have no imagination," stated Darrow at last. "You follow the dictates of rigid science, and of logic."

"Most certainly," Eldridge agreed to this, as to a compliment.

"It takes you far," continued Darrow, "but not far enough. You observe only facts; I also observe men. You will follow only where your facts lead; I am willing to take a leap in the dark. I'll have all this matter hunted out while you are proving your first steps."

"That, I understand it, is a challenge?" demanded Eldridge, touched in his pride of the scientific diagnostician.

The Sign at Six

"That," said Percy Darrow blandly, "is a statement of fact."

"We shall see."

"Sure!" agreed Darrow. "Now, the thing to do is to find Monsieur X. I don't know whether your curiously scutellate mind has arrived at the point where it is willing to admit the existence of Monsieur X or not; but it will. The man who finds Monsieur X wins. Now, you know or can read in the morning paper every fact I have. Go to it!"

Eldridge bowed formally.

"There's one other thing," went on Darrow in a more serious tone of voice. "You have, of course, considered the logical result of this power carried to its ultimate possibility."

"Certainly," replied Eldridge coldly. "The question is superfluous."

"It is a conclusion which many scientific minds will come to, but which will escape the general public unless the surmise is published.

The Sign at Six

For the present I suggest that we use our influence to keep it out of the prints."

Eldridge reflected. "You are quite right," said he; and rose to go.

After his departure Helen turned on Darrow.

"You were positively insulting!" she cried, "and in my house! How could you?"

"Helen," said Darrow, facing her squarely, "I maintained rigidly all the outer forms of politeness. That is as far as I will go anywhere with that man. My statement to him is quite just; he has no humanity."

"What do you mean? Why are you so bitter?" asked Helen, a little subdued in her anger by the young man's evident earnestness.

"You never knew Doctor Schermerhorn, did you, Helen?" he asked.

"The funny little old German? Indeed, I did! He was a dear!"

"He was one of the greatest scientists living

141

The Sign at Six

—and he was a dear! That goes far to explain him—a gentle, wise, child-like, old man—with imagination and a Heaven-seeking soul. He picked me up as a boy, and was a father to me. I was his scientific assistant until he was killed, murdered by the foulest band of pirates. Life passes; and that is long ago."

He fell silent a moment; and the girl looked on this unprecedented betrayal of feeling with eyes at once startled and sympathetic.

"Doctor Schermerhorn," went on Darrow in his usual faintly tired, faintly cynical tone, "worked off and on for five years on a certain purely scientific discovery, the nature of which you would not understand. In conversation he told its essentials to this Eldridge. Doctor Schermerhorn fell sick of a passing illness. When he had recovered, the discovery had been completed and given to the scientific world."

"Oh!" cried Helen. "What a trick!"

"So I think. The discovery was purely theo-

The Sign at Six

retic and brought no particular fame or money to Eldridge. It was, as he looked at it, and as the doctor himself looked at it, merely carrying common knowledge to a conclusion. Perhaps it was; but I never forgave Eldridge for depriving the old man of the little satisfaction of the final proof. It is indicative of the whole man. He lacks humanity, and therefore imagination."

"Still, I wish you wouldn't be quite so bitter when I'm around," pleaded Helen, "though I love your feeling for dear old Doctor Schermerhorn."

"I wish you could arrange to get out of town for a little while," urged Darrow. "Isn't there some one you can visit?"

"Do you mean there is danger?"

"There is the potentiality of danger," Darrow amended. "I am almost confident, if pure reason can be relied on, that when the time comes I can avert the danger."

The Sign at Six

"Almost—" said Helen.

"I may have missed one of the elements of the case—though I do not think so. I can be practically certain when I telephone a man I know—or see the morning papers."

"Telephone now, then. But why 'when the time comes'? Why not now?"

Darrow arose to go to the telephone. He shook his head.

"Let Eldridge do his best. He has always succeeded—triumphantly. Now he will fail, and he will fail in the most spectacular, the most public way possible."

He lifted his eyes, usually so dreamy, so soft brown. Helen was startled at the lambent flash in their depths. He sauntered from the room. After a moment she heard his voice in conversation with the man he had called.

"Hallowell?" he said, "good luck to find you. Did our friend leave on the *Celtic?* No? Sure he didn't sneak off in disguise? I'll trust

"Let Eldridge do his best"

The Sign at Six

you to think of everything. Sure! Meet me at Simmons' wireless in half an hour."

Helen heard the click as he hung up the receiver. A moment later he lounged back into the room.

"All right," he said. "My job's done."

"Done!" echoed Helen in surprise.

"Either I'm right or I'm wrong," said Darrow. "Every element of the game is now certainly before me. If my reasoning is correct I shall receive certain proof of that fact within half an hour. If it is wrong, then I'm away off, and Eldridge's methods will win if any can."

"What is the proof? Aren't you wildly excited? Tell me!" cried Helen.

"The proof is whether or not a certain message has been received over a certain wireless," said Darrow. "I'll know soon enough. But that is not the question; can not you get out of town for a little while?"

145

The Sign at Six

Helen surveyed him speculatively.

"If there is no danger, I can see no reason for it," she stated at length, with decision. "If there is danger you should warn a great many others."

"But if that warning might precipitate the danger?"

"Shall I go or stay?" she demanded, ignoring the equivocation.

Darrow considered.

"Stay," he decided at last. "I'll bet more than my life that I'm right," he muttered. "Now," he continued, a trifle more briskly, "be prepared for fireworks. Unless I'm very much mistaken this little old town is going variously and duly to be stood on its head at odd times soon. That's the way I size it up. Don't be frightened; don't get caught unprepared. I think we've had the whole bag of tricks. At almost any moment we're likely to be cut off from all electricity, all sound, or all light—

The Sign at Six

never more than one at a time. I imagine we shall have ample warning, but perhaps not. In any case, don't be frightened. It's harmless in itself. Better stay home nights. You can reassure your friends if you want to; but on no account get my name in this. If I am quoted, it will do incalculable harm."

"Why not tell the public that it is harmless?" demanded Helen. "Think of the anxiety, the accidents, the genuine terror it would save."

Darrow rose slowly to go. He walked quite deliberately over to Helen, and faced her for a moment in silence.

"Helen," he said impressively at last, "I have talked freely with you because I felt I could trust you. Believe me, I know the exigencies of this case better than you do; and you must obey me in what I say. I am speaking very seriously. If you allow your sympathies to act on the very limited knowledge you possess, you will probably bring about incalculable harm. We walk in safety only while we stick to the path. If you try to act in any case on what your judgment or your sympathies may advise, and without consulting me, you may cause the city, the people, and all that you know or care for to be blotted out of existence. Do you understand? Do you believe me?"

"I understand; I believe you," repeated the girl a trifle faintly.

Darrow left without further ceremony. Helen stood where he had left her on the rug, staring after him, a new expression in her eyes. She had known Percy Darrow for many years. Always she had appreciated his intellect, but deprecated what she had considered his indolence, his softness of character, his tendency to let things drift. For the first time she realized that not invariably do manners make the man.

CHAPTER XIV

THE FEAR OF DANGER

BEFORE leaving the house, Darrow summoned Jack Warford.

"Come on, old bulldog," said he. "You're to live with me a while now. The game is closing down."

"Bully," said Jack. "I'll pack a suit case."

"Have it done for you, and sent down to my place. We must hustle for the Atlas Building now."

"What's doing?" asked Jack, as they boarded a surface car.

"Absolutely nothing—for some time perhaps. But we must be ready. And the waiting will be amusing, I promise you that."

The Sign at Six

When they arrived at the Atlas Building, Darrow was surprised to find Simmons already in charge of the office.

"Thought you were on night duty," said he.

"I am," replied Simmons curtly. "But judging by what you said this morning, I considered I'd better be on the job myself."

"Good boy," approved Darrow. "I see I've made no mistake in you. Just stick it out twelve hours more, and we'll have it settled. Anything more?"

Simmons thrust a message across the table.

Darrow took it quite calmly. At this moment Hallowell entered.

"What time did this come?" asked Darrow, nodding to the reporter.

"At twelve thirty."

Darrow nodded twice with great satisfaction.

Then quite deliberately he unfolded the paper and perused its contents. Without change

150

The Sign at Six

of expression he handed it to Hallowell. The latter read aloud:

"To the People: A traitor is among you—one who has betrayed you, one and all, but whom you cherish to your bosoms as a viper. I, who am greater than you all, have laid my commands upon him, and he has seen fit to disobey He is now in hiding among you. This man must be produced. I would not willingly harass you, but this, my will, must be carried out. If he is not found by six to-morrow a sign will be sent to you that you may believe. I am patient, but I must be obeyed."

"Now, what do you think of that!" cried Hallowell. "He doesn't even mention the name of his friend to the dear people who are to hunt him down! Fine dope!"

Darrow's face expressed a sleepy satisfaction. He stretched his arms and yawned.

"You might supply the deficiency," he suggested. "Well," he remarked to Jack, "that

The Sign at Six

settles it. Everything's running like a catboat in a fair wind. He's in communication with us; he is gaining confidence in his inflated imaginary importance; we are to have a continuance of his peculiar activities; and we can put our hands on him at a moment's notice."

"What!" shouted Hallowell and Jack Warford, leaping to their feet.

"Where is he?" demanded the reporter.

"How do you know?" cried Jack.

Simmons, his head-piece laid aside, looked up at him in silent curiosity.

"It is sufficient for now that I do know," smiled Darrow. "As for how I know, that last wireless proved it to me."

All three men immediately bent over the message for a detailed perusal. After a minute's scrutiny, Hallowell looked up in disappointment.

"Too many for me," he confessed. "What is there in that?"

The Sign at Six

But Darrow shook his head.

"I play my own game," was all the explanation he would vouchsafe.

"You may as well knock off, old man," he told Simmons. "I don't think there'll be anything more doing to-night; and it doesn't matter if there is. Tell your other man to jot down anything from that sending, if any comes. Now," he turned to Hallowell, "I want to see your managing editor."

The three took the subway to City Hall Square. The managing editor received Darrow with much favor as the vehicle of a big scoop brought in far enough ahead of going to press to permit of ample time for its development.

"Now, Mr. Curtis," said Darrow to this man, "this is going to be an interesting week for you. Here's your last exclusive despatch. From to-morrow morning every paper in town will naturally get every wireless that comes in."

The Sign at Six

"H'm," observed Curtis, reading the despatch. "What next?"

"He'll fulfil his threat. To-morrow evening at six o'clock he will stop the vibrations either of light, of electricity, or of sound— probably of electricity, as he has appointed the rush hour."

"Most likely," Curtis agreed.

"Warn the people to keep out of the subways, and not to get scared. Take it easy. There's no danger. Explain why in words of one syllable."

"Sure."

"Now, this is what I'm here for. Up to now these manifestations have been harmless in their direct effects. But follow the hypothesis to its logical conclusion. Suppose this man can arrest the vibrations not only of light and sound, but also of the third member of the vibratory trinity. Suppose he should go one step farther; and, even for the barest fraction of time, should be able to stop the vibrations of heat!"

The managing editor half rose. As the idea in its full significance gained hold on their imaginations the three men turned to stare blankly at one another.

"That is annihilation!" Curtis whispered.

"On a wholesale scale," agreed Darrow calmly. "It means the death of every living thing from the smallest insect to the largest animal, from the microbe to the very lichens on the stones of Trinity. I agree with the way you look." He laughed a little. "But the case isn't so bad as it sounds," he went on. "If the crust of the earth were to collapse, that would be annihilation, too. But it isn't likely to happen. There are several things to think of."

"What, for the love of Pete!" gasped Curtis. "Any small efforts at muck-racking this refrigerator trust would be thankfully received."

"In the first place, as you know," explained

155

The Sign at Six

Darrow, "his power seems to be limited in certain directions. He apparently can stop vibrations only of certain defined wave-lengths at one time. It may be that he is unable to stop heat vibrations at all."

"You'll have to do better than that," growled Curtis.

"The rest is faith—on your part," replied Darrow. "For I'll guarantee that even if Monsieur X has this power, I'll stop him before he exercises it."

"Guarantee?" inquired Curtis.

"There's nothing to prevent my moving to California or Mombassa if I thought myself in any danger here," Darrow pointed out. "It would be very easy for me quietly to warn my friends and quietly do the grand sneak."

"True," muttered Curtis, rummaging on his desk for a pipe.

"The danger isn't the point—*it's the fear of danger*," said Darrow.

The Sign at Six

Curtis looked up, arresting the operation of crowding the tobacco into the pipe bowl.

"Suppose that throughout the length and breadth of this city the idea should be spread broadcast that at any given moment it might be destroyed. Can you imagine the effect?"

"Immediate exodus," grinned Curtis. "Immediate is a nice dignified word," he added.

"Quite so, and then?"

"Eh?"

"What in blazes would four million city people without homes or occupations do? Where would they go? What would happen?"

"You see what I mean," went on Darrow, after the slight pause necessary to let this sink in. "The fear would bring about a general catastrophe only less serious than the fact itself. It's up to you newspaper men to see that they don't catch this fear. There'll be a hundred letters from foxy boys with just enough logic or imagination to see the possibility of cutting off the furnace; but without imagination enough to get the final effect of telling people about it. Suppress it. Unless I'm mistaken, the affair will be over in a week."

Curtis drummed thoughtfully on his desk.

"It's got to be done, and it will be done," he said at last. "I'll get to every paper in the city to-night—if it costs us our scoop."

"But won't the people who write the letters tell about it, anyway?" asked Jack. "And won't the outside papers have the same stuff?"

"Sure," agreed Curtis promptly, "but what isn't in the city press doesn't get to the mass of the public; that's a cinch. There will be some thousands or even tens of thousands who will leave; there'll be rumors a-plenty; there'll be the damnedest row since the Crusades—but the people will stick. I'm taking your word for the danger."

"Well, I'm the hostage," Darrow reminded him.

The Sign at Six

"Correct," said Curtis, reaching for the desk telephone.

Hallowell followed the visitors to the narrow hall.

"Now," said Darrow in parting, "remember what I have said. Don't mention my name nor indicate that there is anywhere an idea that the identity or whereabouts of Monsieur X is by anybody suspected."

CHAPTER XV

HAVING thus detailed rather minutely the situation in which the city and the actors in its drama found themselves, it now becomes necessary to move the action forward to the point where the moneyed interests took a hand in the game.

That was brought about in somewhat more than fifty hours.

In the meantime the facts as to vibrations were published in all the papers; the despatches and the relations between McCarthy and Monsieur X exclusively in the *Despatch*—to that organ's vast satisfaction and credit; and the possibilities of tragedy in none. This latter

The Sign at Six

fact was greatly to the credit of a maligned class of men. It is common belief that no cause is too sacred or no consequence too grave to give pause to the editorial rapacity for news. The present instance disproved that supposition. No journal, yellow or otherwise, contained a line of suggestion that anything beyond annoyance was to be feared from these queer manifestations.

The consequences on a mixed population like that of New York were very peculiar. The people naturally divided themselves into three classes. In the first were those who had received their warning from logic, friends, or the outside world; and who either promptly left town or, being unable to do so, lived in fear. In the second were all that numerous body who, neurasthenically unbalanced or near the overbalance, shut instinctively the eyes of their reason and glowed with a devastating and fanatical religious zeal. Among these, so ex-

The Sign at Six

traordinarily are we constituted, almost immediately grew up various sects, uniting only
in the belief that the wrath of God was upon
an iniquitous people.

By far the largest class of all, comprising
the every-day busy bulk of the people, were
those who accepted the thing at its face value,
read its own papers, went about its business,
and spared time to laugh at the absurdities or
growl at the inconveniences of the phenomena.
With true American adaptability, it speedily
accustomed itself to both the expectation of,
and the coping with, unusual conditions. It
went forth about its daily affairs; it started
for home a little early in order to get there
in season; it eschewed subways and theaters;
it learned to wait patiently, when one of the
three blights struck its world, as a man waits
patiently for a shower to pass.

This class, as has been said, was preponder-
antly in the majority, but its mass was being

The Sign at Six

constantly diminished as a little knowledge of danger seeped into its substance. News of the possible catastrophe passed from mouth to mouth; a world outside, waiting aghast at such fatuity, began to get in its messages. Street-corner alarmists talked to such as would listen. Thousands upon thousands left the city. Hundreds of thousands more, tied hard and fast by the strings of necessity, waited in an hourly growing dread.

The "sign" had been sent promptly at six o'clock, as promised. It proved Darrow's prediction by turning out to be a stoppage of the electrical systems. This time it lasted only half an hour—long enough to throw the traffic and transportation into confusion. It was followed at short intervals by demonstrations in light and sound; none was of long duration.

After the first few, their occurrence came freakishly, in flashes, as though the hidden antagonist delighted in confusing his immense

The Sign at Six

audience. The messages he sent over the wireless in the Atlas Building grew more and more threatening and grandiose. They demanded invariably that McCarthy should be sought out and delivered up to a rather vaguely described vengeance; and threatened with dire calamities all the inhabitants of Manhattan if the Unknown's desires were not fulfilled. These threats grew more definite in character as time went on.

The effect of all this in the long run was, of course, confusion and instability. People laughed or cursed; but they also listened and reasoned. Gradually, throughout the city, dread was extending the blackness of its terror. A knowledge that would have caused a tremendous panic if it had been divulged suddenly now gave birth to a deep-seated uneasiness.

Where the panic would have torn men up by the roots and flung them in terrorized mobs

The Sign at Six

through the congested ways and out into the inhospitable country, the uneasiness of dread held them cowering at their accustomed tasks. They were afraid; but they had had time to think, and they realized what it would mean to leave their beloved or accustomed or necessary city, as the case might be. And it must be remembered that the definite knowledge of what might be feared was not yet disseminated among them.

But this attitude hurt business, and business struck back. The subways were practically deserted; the theaters empty; the accustomed careless life of the Great White Way thinned; the streams of life slackened. Furthermore, the intelligent criminal immediately discovered that ideal shields were being provided him gratis behind which to conduct his crimes. In the silence a man could blow out the side of a bank building with impunity, provided only he kept out of sight. In the darkness he could

The Sign at Six

pilfer at will, with only the proviso that he forget not his gum shoes. The possibilities of night crime when electricity lacks have already been touched upon.

To meet unusual conditions the people individually and collectively rose to heights of forgotten ingenuity. The physical life of a city is so well established that the average city dweller grows out of the pioneer virtue of adaptability. Now once more these people were forced to meet new and untried conditions, to guard against new dangers, new opposing forces. In an incredibly short space of time they grew out of aimless panic. They learned to sit tight; to guard adequately their lives, their treasure, and even to a certain extent their time against undue loss.

In the meantime the moneyed powers had been prompt to act. They did not intend to stand idly while their pockets were being picked by untoward circumstances; nor did

166

The Sign at Six

they intend to continue indefinitely the unusual expenditures necessary to guard themselves against even a greater loss. As there seemed to be two men to find, they employed the best of detectives to search for McCarthy; and Professor Eldridge, as the greatest living expert, to hunt down the Unknown. Thus unexpectedly Eldridge found himself with definite backing in his strange duel with Darrow.

It is now desirable to place before the reader samples of the messages sent by Monsieur X and received in the wireless office of the Atlas Building, after which we can proceed once more to follow out the sequence of events.

"To the People: The sign has been sent you. You must now believe. The traitor is among you, and you must hunt him down. This is your sacred duty, for I, your master, have laid it upon you."

That was one of the first. After a round dozen of similar import, there came this:

The Sign at Six

"To THE PEOPLE: I, your master, am displeased with you. The visitations of darkness and of silence have been sent, but you have heeded little. I doubt not that ye search, as I have commanded, but you do not realize to the full your sacred obligation. You go about your business and you carry on your affairs. Your business and your affairs are not so important as these, my commands. Beware lest you draw down the wrath of the Lord's Anointed. I am patient with your ignorance; but give heed."

The last at present to which your attention is called came just before the events to be detailed:

"To THE PEOPLE: Your time is drawing short. You are a stubborn and a stiff-necked generation. My patience is ebbing away. You have been shown the power of my right hand, and you have gone your accustomed ways. You have defied the might of the Right Hand of God. Now I will lay on you my commands.

The Sign at Six

You must seek out Apollyon and deliver him even into my hands, and that shortly. I shall be patient yet a little while longer, for I know that you grope in darkness and have not the light that shines upon me. But soon I shall strike."

CHAPTER XVI

THE PROFESSOR'S EXPERIMENT

THROUGHOUT all this excitement Percy Darrow did absolutely nothing. He spent all his time, save that required for meals and the shortest necessary sleep, in a round-armed wooden chair in the wireless station of the Atlas Building. Jack Warford sat with him. Darrow rarely opened his mouth for speech, but smoked slowly a few cigarettes, and rolled many more, which he held unlighted in the corner of his mouth until they dropped to pieces. He watched quietly all that went on; glanced through such messages as came in from Monsieur X, read the papers, and dozed. To reporters he was affable enough in his drawling slow fashion, but had nothing to say.

The Sign at Six

"Eldridge is doing this," he said to them; "I'm only in the position of an interested spectator."

Eldridge had taken hold in a thoroughly competent way. Back of the cold precision of his undoubted scientific attainments lurked, unexpected by most, a strong ambition and a less admirable hankering for the lime-light. His opportunity to gratify all these appetites—science, advancement, and fame—was too good not to cause him the deepest satisfaction.

"I have determined," he told the reporters, "that this particular instrument alone receives the messages from the unknown perpetrator. Our investigations must be initiated, therefore, in this apartment."

"How do you explain it?" asked one of the reporters.

"I can not explain it scientifically," admitted Eldridge, "but I can surmise that the fact either purposely or accidentally has to do either

171

The Sign at Six

with this instrument's location or with some slight and undetermined peculiarity of its tuning."

"You could easily tell which by moving the instrument to another station where they aren't getting the messages now," suggested Darrow lazily.

"Certainly," snapped Eldridge, "any child could deduce that. But I fail to see the use or necessity for the determination at all—unless in a spirit of frivolous play. Our task is not to discover where the messages can be received, but whence they are sent."

He gazed frostily at the man who had interrupted him. Darrow smiled softly back.

"How far will your instrument carry in sending?" Eldridge asked Simmons.

"Its extreme is about two hundred miles."

"Then we can safely assume that a circle drawn with a two-hundred-mile radius would contain this man you call Monsieur X"—the

The Sign at Six

newspapers had adopted Darrow's nickname for the Unknown—"since you have succeeded in communicating with him."

"Marvelous," said Darrow to Jack—but under his breath.

"As the sending of Monsieur X is faint, it follows that he is somewhere near the periphery of this circle, or that he is possessed of a primitive or weak instrument. By the doctrine of probabilities we should be justified in concluding against the latter supposition."

"How's that, Professor?" asked the *Morning Register* man. "It doesn't get to me."

"He is evidently a man not only of scientific attainments, but of immense scientific possessions—as is evidenced by these phenomenal results he is able to accomplish. But we are not justified in reasoning according to the doctrine of probabilities. Therefore, we shall proceed methodically. I have already made my preparations."

The Sign at Six

Eldridge looked about him with an air of triumph.

"I am fortunate enough to have, in the present crisis, unlimited financial backing," he said. "Therefore, I am in a position to carry out the most exhaustive of experiments."

He stretched his hand out for a long roll, which he laid flat upon the table, pinning down the corners.

"Here is a map of the Eastern States," said he. "I have drawn a circle on it with a two-hundred-miles radius. At this moment a private instrument with a full crew to string sending and receiving wires is two hundred miles from here on the New York Central Railroad. It has for its transportation a private train, and it will be given a clear right of way." He turned to Simmons. "Have you found yourself able to communicate with this Monsieur X at any time?"

"Communicate!" echoed Simmons. "Why,

The Sign at Six

he's easier to talk to than a girl who wants an ice-cream soda!"

"Then send this: 'Your messages have been communicated to the people. Be patient.'"

Simmons touched the key. The spark leaped crashing.

"What do you get?" asked Eldridge, after a moment.

"Oh, a lot of the same sort of dope," answered Simmons wearily. "Do you want it?"

"No, it is not necessary," replied Eldridge. "But listen for another message from about the same distance when he has finished."

Silence fell on the room. At the end of ten minutes Simmons raised his head.

"I get 'O K Q' over and over," said he. "Want that?"

"That," replied Eldridge with satisfaction, "indicates that my crew on the special train in the Adirondacks two hundred miles away has heard your message to Monsieur X." He

175

The Sign at Six

glanced at his watch. "Now, if you would be so good as to afford me a moment's assistance," he requested Simmons, "I wish to disconnect from your battery one of your powerful Leyden jars, and to substitute for it one of weaker voltage. I ventured to instruct my delivery man to leave a few in the outer hall."

"That will weaken the sending power of my instrument," objected Simmons.

"Exactly what I wish to do," replied Eldridge.

"He's clever all right," Darrow murmured admiringly to Jack. "See what he's up to?"

"Not yet," muttered Jack.

The substitution completed, Eldridge again glanced at his watch.

"Now," he instructed Simmons, "send the letters 'Q E D,' and continue to do so until you again hear the letters 'O K Q.'"

Simmons set himself to the task. It was a long one. At last he reported his answer.

The Sign at Six

"He sends 'O K Q ten,'" he said.

Eldridge turned to the reporters.

"That means that the substitution of the smaller Leyden jar for one of the larger reduced the sending power of this instrument just ten miles," said he. "My crew has quite simply moved slowly forward until it caught our sending here."

"Next," he instructed Simmons, "see if you can communicate with Monsieur X."

The operator speedily reported his success at that. Eldridge removed his glasses and polished their lenses.

"Thus, gentlemen," said he, "from our circle of two-hundred-mile radius we have eliminated a strip ten miles wide. Naturally if this weakened sending reaches only one hundred and ninety miles, and our antagonist receives our messages, he must be nearer than one hundred and ninety miles. We will now further reduce the strength of our sending and try again."

The Sign at Six

The younger men present broke into a shout.
"Good work!" somebody cried. They
crowded about, keenly interested in this new
method of man-hunting. Only Darrow, tipped
back in his chair against the wall, seemed un-
excited.

To Jack's whispered question he shook his
head.

"It's ingenious," he acknowledged, "but he's
on the wrong track." That was as far as he
would explain, and soon dropped into a slight
doze.

Throughout the greater part of the night the
experiment continued. Battery by battery the
sending power of the instrument was weakened. Mile by mile the special train drew
nearer until, by catching the prearranged signal, it determined just how far the new sending
reached. Then Simmons tried Monsieur X.
As the latter invariably answered, it was, of
course, evident that he remained still in the

The Sign at Six

narrowing zone of communication. ᐟ It was fascinating work, like the drawing of a huge invisible net.

The reporters on the morning papers mastered only with difficulty their inclination to stay. They had to leave before their papers went to press, but were back again in an hour, unwilling to lose a moment of the game. A tension vibrated the little office. Only Percy Darrow dozed alone in the corner, leaning back in his wooden armchair.

At near four o'clock in the morning Simmons raised his head after a long bout of calling to announce that he could get no reply from Monsieur X.

"He's got tired of your fool messages," remarked the *Register* man. "And I don't wonder! Guess he's gone to bed."

Eldridge said nothing, but replaced the Leyden jar he had but just removed.

"Try one," said he.

The Sign at Six

"I get him," reported Simmons, after a moment.

"Send him anything plausible and reassuring," commanded Eldridge hastily. He turned to his small and attentive audience in triumph. "Thus, gentlemen," he announced, "we have proven conclusively that our man is located between forty and fifty miles from New York. If we draw two circles, with this building as center, the circumference of one of which is fifty, the other forty miles away, we define the territory within which the malefactor in question is to be found."

The people in the room crowded close about the table to examine the map upon which Professor Eldridge had drawn the circles.

"There's an awful lot of country—some of it pretty wild," objected the *Bulletin* man. "It will be a long job to hunt a man down in that territory."

"Even if it were as extensive a task as a

The Sign at Six

hasty review of the facts might indicate," stated Eldridge, "I venture to assert that enough men would be forthcoming to expedite such a search. But modifying circumstances will lighten the task."

"How's that?" asked the *Banner* man, speaking for the others' evident interest.

"We have no means of surmising the method by which this man succeeds in arresting vibratory motions of certain wave-lengths," said Eldridge didactically, "any more than we are able to define the precise nature of electricity. But, as in the case of electricity, we can observe the action of its phenomena. Two salient features leap out at us: one is that these phenomena are limited in time; the other that they are limited in space. The latter aspect we will examine, if you please, gentlemen.

"The phenomena have been directed with great accuracy (a) at the Atlas Building; **(b) at** this city and some of its immediate

The Sign at Six

suburbs. The peculiarity of this can not but strike an observant mind. How is this man able, at forty or fifty miles distance, to concentrate his efforts on one comparatively small objective? We can only surmise some system of insulating screens or focal mirrors. I might remark in passing that the existence of this power to direct or focus the more rapid ethereal vibrations would be a discovery of considerable scientific moment. But if this is the method employed, why do we not cut a band of vibratory nullifications, rather than touch upon a focal point?"

"Repeat softly," murmured the irrepressible *Register* man.

"Why," explained Eldridge patiently, "are not the people and buildings between here and the unknown operator affected? The only hypothesis we are justified in working upon is that the man's apparatus is at a height sufficient to carry over intervening obstacles. This hy-

The Sign at Six

pothesis is strengthened by the collateral fact
that the territory we have just determined as
that within which he must be found lies in the
highlands of our own and neighboring states.
We may, therefore, eliminate the low-lying
districts within our radius."

Percy Darrow opened one eye.

"Perhaps he's up in a balloon," he drawled
languidly; "better take along an aeroplane."

Eldridge cast on him a look of cold scorn.
Darrow closed the eye.

CHAPTER XVII

DRAWING THE NET

THE "zone of danger", as the *Bulletin* named it, was immediately the scene of swarming activities. Besides the expedition immediately despatched by the interests backing the investigation, several enterprising newspapers saw a fine chance for a big scoop, and sent out much-heralded parties of their own. The activities of these were well reported, you may be sure. Public interest was at once focused reassuringly on the chances of finding the annoying malefactor to-day or to-morrow; there no longer existed a doubt that he would be found. The weight of dread was lifted,

184

The Sign at Six

and in the reaction people made light of the inconveniences and fun of the menacing messages that now came in by the dozen.

It was necessary to take extraordinary precautions against thieves and fire; the people took them. It was needful to slacken business in order that the congestion of the rush hour might not again prove tragic; business was slackened. People were willing to undergo many things, because, after all, they were but temporary. The madman of the Catskills would sooner or later be found; his pernicious activities brought to a conclusion. The country to be searched was tremendous, of course, but the search was thorough.

The public delivered itself joyously to a debauch of rumors and of "extras". The insistent alarms of danger, trickling in slowly from the outside world, dried up in the warmth of optimism. Only the more thoughtful, to a few of whom these warnings came, coupled

The Sign at Six

them with Monsieur X's repeated threats, and walked uncertain and in humility.

Percy Darrow did not interest himself in the search, nor did he desert his post in the wireless office. There he did nothing whatever. Jack Warford stayed with him, but immensely bored, it must be confessed. Once he suggested that if Darrow had nothing for him to do that afternoon, he thought he would like to go out for a little exercise.

Darrow shook his head.

"You may go, if you want to, Jack," said he, "but if you do I'll have to get some one else. This isn't much of a job, but I may need you any moment."

"All right," agreed Jack cheerfully. "Only I wish you'd let a fellow know what to expect."

Darrow shook his head. The two now practically lived in the office. Neither had taken his clothes off for several days. They slept in their chairs or on the lounge. Darrow read the

The Sign at Six

various messages from the Unknown, glanced over the newspapers, and dozed.

Thus there passed two days of the search. On the third day the intermittent phenomena and the messages suddenly ceased. This fact was hailed jubilantly by all the papers as indicating that at last the quarry had become alarmed by the near-coming search. From the contracted district still remaining to be combed over, nobody was permitted to depart; and so closely was the cordon drawn by so large a posse that it was physically impossible for any living being to slip by the line.

Thus even if Monsieur X, convinced that at last his discovery was imminent, should destroy his apparatus or attempt to move it and himself to a place of safety, he would find his escape cut off. Thousands of men were employed, and thousands more drafted in as volunteers to render this outcome assured.

It was an army deployed in an irregular cir-

cle, and moving inward toward its center. Men
of the highest executive ability commanded it,
saw to its necessary deliberation, eliminated all
possibility of a confusion through which any
man could slip. The occasion was serious, and
it was taken seriously.

Of the outcome no one in touch with the
situation had a moment's doubt. The messages
and the phenomena had continued to come
from the danger zone. It was of course evident that they could not have been sent from
any portion of the zone actually searched and
occupied by the searchers. The remaining portion of the zone, from which they were still
coming, had been completely surrounded.
After that the manifestations had ceased.
Therefore, Monsieur X must be within the be-
leaguered circle. To add to the probabilities,
as Eldridge pointed out, the remaining district
compassed the highest hills in the zone—a fact
on all fours with his hypothesis.

The Sign at Six

On the appointed morning the army moved toward the center. Men beat the ground carefully, so close to one another that they could touch hands. As they closed in the ranks became thicker. Animals of many kinds, confused as the ranks closed in on them, tried to break through the cordon and were killed. Captains held order in the front row, that the army might not become a crowd. Birds, alarmed by the shouting, rose and wheeled.

In the city immense crowds watched the bulletins sent momently from the very field itself by private wires strung hastily for the occasion. Enterprising journals had prepared huge rough maps, on which the contracting circle was indicated by red lines, constantly redrawn. It was discovery before a multitude. The imagination of the public, fired by its realization of this fact, stretched itself ahead of the distant beaters, bodying forth what they might find.

The Sign at Six

As the circle narrowed excitement grew. All business ceased. The streets were crowded; the windows of the buildings looking out on the numerous bulletin-boards were black with heads. Those who could not see demanded eagerly of those who could.

In the Atlas Building the wireless operator hung out of his window. Beside him was Jack Warford.

Darrow declined to join them. "You tell me," said he.

Jack therefore reported back over his shoulder the bulletins as they appeared. The crowds below read them, their faces upturned. One ran:

"Cordon now has surrounded the crest of the Knob. Station of Monsieur X determined among oak-trees. Men halted. Picket company surrounds."

The crowd roared its appreciation and impa-

The Sign at Six

tience. A long pause followed. Then came the next bulletin:

"Search discovers nothing."

A puzzled angry murmur arose, confused and chopped, like cross currents in a tideway. Finally this was hung out:

"No traces of human occupancy."

A moment's astonished pause ensued. Then, over the vast multitude, its faces upturned in incredulous amazement; over the city lying sparkling in the noonday sun fell the pall of absolute darkness.

In the wireless office of the Atlas Building Percy Darrow laughed.

CHAPTER XVIII

CONFUSION WORSE CONFOUNDED

THE absolute failure of Eldridge's hypothesis immediately threw public confidence into a profound reaction. Certainty gave place to complete distrust. Rumor gained ground. The exodus increased. Where formerly only those who could do so without great sacrifice or inconvenience had left town, now people were beginning to cut loose at any cost. Men resigned their positions in order to get their families away; others began to arrange their affairs as best they might, as though for a long vacation. As yet panic had not appeared openly in the light of day, but she lurked in the shadows of men's hearts.

The Sign at Six

The railroads and steamboats were crowded beyond their capacity. Extra trains followed one another as close together as the block signals would allow them to run. Humanity packed the cars. It was like a continual series of football days. In three of them it was estimated that two hundred thousand people had left Manhattan. It would have been physically impossible for the transportation lines to have carried a thousand more. They had reached their capacity; the spigot was wide open.

Percy Darrow showed Jack the head-lines to this effect.

"Cheerful thought," he suggested. "Suppose the whole four million should want to get out at the same time!"

Eldridge had come back to the wireless office thoroughly bewildered. It is a well-known fact that the exact scientist is the hardest man to fool, but the most fooled if fooled at all. Witness the extent to which noted scientists

193

The Sign at Six

have been taken in by faking spiritualist me-
diums. So with Eldridge. His hypothesis
had been so carefully worked out that the failure of its logic threw his mind into confusion.
Until he could discover the weak link in his
chain of reasoning, that confusion must continue.

An hour and a half after the bulletin an-
nouncing the failure of the search had been
posted, Eldridge rushed into the wireless office.
The plague of darkness had lifted after fifteen
minutes' duration.

"Call Monsieur X," he gasped to the day
operator. In fifteen minutes, by rapid substi-
tutions of batteries to weaken or strengthen
the sending current, he had redetermined his
previous data. Apparently, without the shadow
of a doubt, Monsieur X was within the circle.

"He may be at sea," suggested the operator.

But Eldridge shook his head. The circle of
the sea had been well patrolled, and for days.

The Sign at Six

"Begin over again," drawled Darrow. "I told you that you were on the wrong track."

Eldridge glanced at him.

"I can't say that you've done much!" said he tartly.

"No?" queried Darrow, with one of his slow and exasperating smiles. "Perhaps not. But you'd better get to thinking. You won't be able always to take things easy. You may have to hustle before long."

"There has been, I admit," said Eldridge stiffly, repeating in substance the interview he had already given out, "some flaw in our chain of reasoning. This it will be necessary to review with the object of revision. Every physical manifestation must have some physical and definite cause; and this can be found if time enough is bestowed on it. Often the process of elimination is the only method by which the truth can be determined."

Darrow chuckled.

The Sign at Six

"Look out the process of elimination doesn't overtake you," he remarked.

Eldridge detailed the same reasoning, at greater length, to the men who had employed him. These were very impatient. Business was being not merely impeded, but destroyed. Their customers had no time for them; their employees were in many cases leaving their jobs. They called in all the help they could to assist Eldridge's speculations, but in the end they had to fall back on the scientist as the best on the market. The case was not left in his hands alone, however. After a meeting they offered a reward to any one discovering and putting to an end the disconcerting phenomena.

"Here's where we make money, Jack, big money," observed Darrow when he read this offer. "It'll be bigger before we get through. You and I can have the little expedition to Volcano Island."

The Sign at Six

"Nothing suits me better," said Jack. "Are you sure we'll get it?"

"Sure," said Darrow.

Monsieur X had of course honored the waiting world with a message. It followed the fifteen minutes of darkness:

"To THE PEOPLE: I have been patient and have stayed my hand in order that you may learn the vanity of your endeavor. Who are ye that ye shall strive to take me? Vanity and foolishness is your portion. Now ye know my power and ye will listen unto my words as to the words of the Master. Ye must hunt down this man McCarthy and deliver him over unto me. If every one of you gives himself to the task, lo! it is quickly done. Bestir yourselves against the wrath to come!"

These events occupied the three days of the ordered exodus. The time was further filled with rumor that ever grew more dire. Gradually business was supended entirely. Those

The Sign at Six

who could not or would not go away stood about talking matters over, and, as is always the case, matters did not improve in the telling. The only activity in the city was that bent on seeking out the abiding-place of Monsieur X.

Eldridge had now come to the conclusion that he had perhaps been mistaken in confining his efforts to so small an area. In fact, further experiments rendered hazy the arbitrary outlines formerly determined for the zone of danger. At times Monsieur X answered well within the forty-five-mile mark; at times somewhat beyond the end of the fifty-mile radius. Eldridge immediately undertook a series of more delicate experiments by means of indicators especially designed by him for the occasion. Once more the little wireless office became the focus of reportorial attention.

"Our major premises we find still to be correct," announced Eldridge in the coldly didactic manner characteristic of the man. "This

The Sign at Six

unknown operator is at a distance; and probably at a height. One indication we did not take sufficiently into consideration—the fact that this instrument alone is capable of communication with the instrument of this individual."

Percy Darrow for the first time began to show signs of attention. He dropped the legs of his chair to the floor and leaned forward.

"That would indicate, gentlemen, that the instrument whose location we are desirous of determining is of a peculiar nature. What that nature is we have no means of determining accurately; but in conjunction with the fact that our previous experiments failed to locate Monsieur X, we may adopt the hypothesis that the wireless apparatus of that individual is not so delicately responsive as the average. In other words, the zone within which he may be found is in fact wider than we had supposed."

The Sign at Six

Darrow leaned back against the wall and closed his eyes. Eldridge continued, explaining the means he had taken to determine more accurately the exact location of Monsieur X.

CHAPTER XIX

PERCY KEEPS VIGIL

THE morning of the third day after the failure of the search, and of the sixth since McCarthy's disappearance, had arrived. During that time Percy Darrow, apparently insensible to fatigue, had maintained an almost sleepless vigil. His meals Jack Warford brought in to him; he dozed in his chair or on the couch. Never did he appear to do anything.

The very persistent quietude of the man ended by making its impression. To all questions, however, Darrow returned but the one reply, delivered always in a voice full of raillery:

The Sign at Six

"I couldn't bear to miss a single step of Eldridge's masterly work."

About half past nine of the morning in question, through the door to the wireless office, always half opened, somebody looked hesitatingly into the room. Instantly Darrow and Jack were on their feet and in the hallway.

"Helen!" cried Jack.

"What is it? Anything happened?" demanded Darrow.

She surveyed them both amusedly.

"You certainly look like a frowzy tramp, Jack," she told her brother judiciously, "and you need sleep," she informed Darrow.

The young scientist bowed ironically, his long lashes drooping over his eyes in his accustomed lazy fashion as he realized that the occasion was not urgent. Helen turned directly to him.

"When are you going to stop this?" she demanded.

The Sign at Six

Darrow raised his eyebrows.

"You needn't look at me like that. You said you could lay your hands on Monsieur X at any moment; why don't you do it?"

"Eldridge is too amusing."

"Too amusing!" echoed the girl. "All you think of is yourself."

"Is it?" drawled Darrow.

"Have you been out in the city? Have you seen the people? Have you seen men out of work? Families leaving their homes? Panic spreading slowly but surely over a whole city?"

"Those pleasures have been denied me," said Darrow blandly.

The girl looked at him with bright angry eyes. Her cheeks were glowing, and her whole figure expressed a tense vibrant life in singular contrast to the apparent indolence of the men at whom she was talking.

"You are insufferable!" She fairly stamped her foot in vexation. "You are an egoist!

The Sign at Six

You would play with the welfare of four million people to gratify your little personal desire for getting even!"

"Steady, sis!" warned Jack.

Darrow had straightened, and his indolent manner had fallen from him.

"I have said I would permit no harm to come to these people, and I mean it," said he.

"No harm!" cried Helen. "What do you call this—"

Darrow turned to the window looking out over the city.

"This!" he said. "Why, this isn't harm! There isn't a man out there who is not better off for what has happened to him. He has lost a little time, a little money, a little sleep, and he has been given a new point of view, a new manhood. As a city dweller he was becoming a mollusk, a creature that could not exist without its shell. The city transported him, warmed him, fed him, amused him, protected

The Sign at Six

him. He had nothing to do with it in any way; he didn't even know how it was done. Deprived of his push-buttons, he was as helpless as a baby. Beyond the little stunt he did in his office or his store, and beyond the ability to cross a crowded street, he was no good. He not only didn't know how to do things, but he was rapidly losing, through disuse, the power to learn how to do things. The modern city dweller, bred, born, brought up on this island, is about as helpless and useless a man, considered as a four-square, self-reliant individual, as you can find on the broad expanse of the globe. I've got no use for a man who can't take care of himself, who's got to have somebody else to do it for him, whenever something to which he hasn't been accustomed rises up in front of him!"

His eye was fixed somberly on the city stretching away into the haze of the autumn day.

The Sign at Six

"You blame me for letting this thing run!"
he went on. "Of course it tickles me to death
to see Eldridge flounder; but that isn't all.
This is the best thing that could happen to
them out there! I'm just patriotic enough to
wish them more of it. It's good medicine! At
last every man jack of them is up against
something he's got to decide for himself. The
police are useless; the fire department is useless; the railroads and street-cars are crippled.
If a man is going to take care of his life and
property, he must do it himself. He's buying
back his self-reliance. Self-reliance is a valu-
able property. He ought to pay something for
it. Generally he has to pay war or insurrection
or bloody riot. In the present instance he's
getting off cheap."

He turned back from the open window. His
eye traveled beyond Helen's trim figure down
the empty hall. "Wait right here, Jack," he
shot over his shoulder, and rushed along the

The Sign at Six

hall and down the stairway before either the young man or his sister could recover from their astonishment.

CHAPTER XX

THE PLAGUE OF COLD

WITHOUT pause, and three steps at a time, Darrow ran down three flights of stairs. Then, recovering from his initial excitement somewhat, he caught the elevator and shot to the street. There he walked rapidly to the subway, which he took as far as City Hall Square. On emerging from the subway station he started across for the *Despatch* office as fast as he could walk. By the entrance to the City Hall, however, he came to an abrupt halt. From the open doorway rushed his friend, Officer Burns, of the City Hall Station.

The policeman's face was chalky white; his eyes were staring, his cap was over one side, he

208

The Sign at Six

staggered uncertainly. As he caught sight of Darrow he stumbled to the young man and clung to his neck, muttering incoherently. People passing in and out looked at him curiously and smiled.

"My God!" gasped Burns, his eyes roving. "I says to him, 'Mike, I don't wonder you've got cold feet.' And there he was, and the mayor—Heaven save—and his secretary! My God!"

Darrow shook his shoulder.

"Here," he said decisively, "what are you talking about? Get yourself together! Remember you're an officer; don't lose your nerve this way!"

At the touch to his pride Burns did pull himself together somewhat, but went on under evident strong excitement.

"I went in just now to the mayor's office a minute," said he, "and saw my friend Mike Mallory, the doorkeeper, settin' in his chair, as

The Sign at Six

usual. It was cold-like, and I went up to him and says, 'Mike, no wonder you get cold feet down here,' just by way of a joke; and when he didn't answer, I went up to him, and he was dead, there in his chair!"

"Well, you've seen dead men before. There's no occasion to lose your nerve, even if you did know him," said Darrow.

The brutality of the speech had its intended effect. Burns straightened.

"That's all very well," said he more collectively. *"But the man was froze!"*

"Frozen!" muttered Darrow, and whistled.

"Yes, and what's more, his little dog, setting by the chair, was froze, too; so when I stepped back sudden and hit against him, he tumbled over *bang*, like a cast-iron dog! That got my goat! I ran!"

"Come with me," ordered Darrow decisively.

They entered the building and ran up the

The Sign at Six

single flight of stairs to the second-story room
which the mayor of that term had fitted up as a
sort of private office of his own. A sharp chill
hung in the hallways; this increased as they
neared the executive's office. Outside the door
sat the doorkeeper in his armchair. Beside
him was a dog, in the attitude of an animal
seated on its haunches, but lying on its side,
one fore leg sticking straight out. Darrow
touched the man and stooped over to peer in
his face. The attitude was most lifelike; the
color was good. A deadly chill ran from Darrow's finger tips up his arm.

He pushed open the door cautiously and
looked in.

"All right, Burns," said he. "The atmosphere has become gaseous again. We can go
in." With which strange remark he entered
the room, followed closely, but uncertainly by
the officer.

The private office possessed the atmosphere

The Sign at Six

of a cold-storage vault. Four men occupied it. At the desk was seated the mayor, leaning forward in an attitude of attention, his triple chin on one clenched fist, his heavy face scowling in concentration. Opposite him lounged two men, one leaning against the table, the other against the wall. One had his hand raised in argument, and his mouth open. The other was watching, an expression of alertness on his sharp countenance. At a typewriter lolled the clerk, his hand fumbling among some papers.

The group was exceedingly lifelike, more so, Darrow thought, than any wax figures the Eden Musée had ever placed for the mystification of its country visitors. Indeed, the only indication that the men had not merely suspended action on the entrance of the visitors was a fine white rime frost that sparkled across the burly countenance of the mayor. Darrow remembered that, summer and winter, that dignitary had always perspired!

The Sign at Six

Burns stood by the door, rooted to the spot, his jaw dropped, his eye staring. Darrow quite calmly walked to the desk. He picked up the inkstand and gazed curiously at its solidified contents, touched the nearest man, gazed curiously at the papers on the desk, and addressed Burns.

"These seem to be frozen, too," he remarked almost sleepily, "and about time, too. This is a sweet gang to be getting together on this sort of a job!"

Quite calmly he gathered the papers on the desk and stuffed them into his pocket. He picked up the desk telephone, giving a number. "Ouch, this receiver's cold," he remarked to Burns. "Hello, *Despatch*. Is Hallowell in the office? Just in? Send him over right quick, keen jump, City Hall, mayor's second-story office. No, right now. Tell him it's Darrow."

He hung up the receiver.

"Curious phenomenon," he remarked to

213

The Sign at Six

Burns, who still stood rooted to the spot. "You see, their bodies were naturally almost in equilibrium, and, as they were frozen immediately, that equilibrium was maintained. And the color. I suppose the blood was congealed in the smaller veins, and did not, as in more gradual freezing, recede to the larger blood-vessels. I'm getting frost bitten myself in here. Let's get outside."

But Officer Burns heard none of this. As Darrow moved toward the door he crossed himself and bolted. Darrow heard his heels clattering on the cement of the corridors. He smiled.

"And now the deluge!" he remarked.

The crowds, terrified, inquisitive, sceptical, and speculative, gathered. Officials swept them out and took possession. Hallowell and Darrow conferred earnestly together.

"He has the power to stop heat vibrations, you see," Darrow said. "That makes him really dangerous. His activities here are in line with his other warnings; but he is not ready to go to extremes yet. The city is yet safe."

"Why?" asked Hallowell.

"I know it. But he has the power. If he gets dangerous we must stop him."

"You are sure you can do it?"

"Sure."

"Then, for God's sake, do it! Don't you realize what will happen when news of this gets out, and people understand what it means? Don't you feel your guilt at those men's deaths?" He struck his hand in the direction of the City Hall.

"The people will buy a lot of experience, at cost of a little fright and annoyance," replied Percy Darrow carelessly. "It'll do them good. When it's over, they'll come back again and be good. As for that bunch in there—when you look over those papers I think you'll be inclined

The Sign at Six

to agree with what the religious fanatics will say—that it was a visitation of God."

"But the old, the sick—there'll be deaths among them—the responsibility is something fearful—"

"Never knew a battle fought yet without some loss," observed Darrow.

Hallowell was staring at him.

"I don't understand you," said the reporter. "You have no heart. You are as bad as this Monsieur X, and between you you hold a city in your power—one way or the other!"

"Well, I rather like being a little god," remarked Darrow.

Hallowell started once more to plead, but Darrow cut him short.

"You are thinking of the present," he said. "I am thinking of the future. It's a good thing for people to find out that there's something bigger than they are, or than anything they can make. That fact is the basis of the

The Sign at Six

idea of a God. These are getting to be a god-less people." He turned on Hallowell, his sleepy eyes lighting up. "I should be very sorry if I had not intellect enough and imagination enough to see what this may mean to my fellow people; and I should despise myself if I should let an unrestrained compassion lose to four million people the rare opportunity vouchsafed them."

He spoke very solemnly. Hallowell looked at him puzzled.

"Besides," said Darrow whimsically, "I like to devil Eldridge."

He dove into the subway. Hallowell gazed after him.

"There goes either a great man or a crazy fool," he remarked to an English sparrow. He turned over rapidly the papers Darrow had found on the mayor's desk, and smiled grimly. "Of all the barefaced, bald-headed steals!" he said.

The Sign at Six

Darrow soon mounted once more the elevator of the Atlas Building. He found Jack and Helen still waiting. Before entering the wireless office Darrow cast a scrutinizing glance along the empty hall.

"It's all right," he said. "I'm surer than ever. Everything fits exactly. Now, Helen," he said, "I want you to go home, and I want you to stay there. No matter what happens, do not move from the house. This town is going to have the biggest scare thrown into it that any town ever had since Sodom and Gomorrah got their little jolt. In the language of the Western prophet, 'Hell will soon be popping.' Let her pop. Sit tight; tell your friends to sit tight. If necessary, tell them Monsieur X is captured, and all his works. Tell them I said so."

His air of languid indifference had fallen from him. His eye was bright, and he spoke with authority and vigor.

218

The Sign at Six

"You take her home, Jack," he commanded, "and return here at once. Don't forget that nice new-blued pop-gun of yours; we're coming to the time when we may need it."

Jack rose instantly to his mood.

"Correct, General!" he saluted. "Where'd you collect the plunder?" he asked, pointing to a square black bag of some size that Darrow had brought back with him.

"That," said Darrow, "is the first fruit of my larcenous tendencies. I stole that from the mayor's office in the City Hall."

"What is it?"

"That," said Darrow, "I do not know."

He deposited the bag carefully by his chair, and turned, smiling, to Helen.

"Good-by," said he. "Sleep tight."

They went out. Darrow seated himself in his chair, drew his hat over his eyes, and fell into a doze. In the meantime, outside, all through the city, hell was getting ready to pop.

CHAPTER XXI

IN THE FACE OF ETERNITY

HELL popped just as soon as the newspapers could get out their extras. Monsieur X had at last struck, and both interest and belief urged the managing editors at last to give publicity to all the theories, the facts, and the latest message from the fanatic Unknown.

The latter came about three o'clock:

"To THE PEOPLE: You have defied me, and you have doubted my power. There is no good in you. I, who would have saved you, now must bring about your death as a stubborn and a stiff-necked generation. In humanity is no more good, and of this world I desire nothing more. Prepare within the next three hours to appear before a mightier throne than mine."

220

The Sign at Six

Percy Darrow, reading this, said to Jack Warford, "It is time to act," and, accompanied by the younger man, quietly left the room.

The reader of imagination—and no other will read this tale—must figure to himself the island of Manhattan during the next two hours. The entire population, nearly, tried to leave it at once. When only the suburban dwellers, urged simply by the desire for a hot dinner, attempt to return home between five and six, the ways are congested enough. Now, stricken with the fear of death, the human cattle fought frantically to reach the inadequate exits of the great theater of tragedy.

There was fighting in the streets, and panic, and stark rumor, of course; and there was heroism, and coolness, and the taking of thought. To the little group of men in the top floor of the Atlas Building the roar of riot came up like the thunder of the orchestra before the rise of the curtain. Most of the people

The Sign at Six

in the streets fled from a danger they did not understand. This little group in the wireless office realized clearly what still and frozen dissolution the rising of the curtain would disclose. They were not many; and they did not know what they were to do, if anything; but they had not run away.

Eldridge was there, looking somewhat flustered for the first time in his life, and four of the large committee that had employed him. Simmons sat calmly at his post, and of all the reporters Hallowell alone had stood by. He had faith in Darrow, and he knew that in the *Despatch* office a little handful of men stood in the shadow of death on the off chance of the biggest scoop since Noah's flood.

The four solid citizens looked at one another. The oldest turned to Eldridge.

"Then your opinion is that the city is doomed?"

"I can offer no other solution, sir," said the

The Sign at Six

scientist. "It is at last evident that this man's power over ethereal vibrations extends to those forming heat-rays. If this is so, it follows that he can cut off all life by stopping all heat. If his threat is carried out, we can but look forward to a repetition on a large scale of the City Hall affair."

The aged financier now spoke to Simmons.

"And the last report from the searchers?" he asked formally.

"The search is being pushed, sir," replied the operator, "by twenty thousand men. There remain some fifty miles of country to go over, Mr. Lyons."

Lyons turned his shaggy head toward a younger, slim, keen-eyed man of fifty,

"And the city will, in your judgment, Mr. Perkins, take how long to empty?"

"Days—in the present confusion," said Perkins shortly. "We can move only a limited percentage. Thank God, most of our men are

The Sign at Six

standing by. I think all our rolling stock is moving."

Lyons nodded twice.

"And you?" he asked the third of the party, a stout young man of thirty-eight or so.

"How many stations are on the job, Simmons?" asked this man.

"All but two, sir," replied the operator. "D and P don't answer. I guess they beat it."

"How do they report the bulletin men?"

"On the job," replied the wireless man.

The stout young man turned to Lyons.

"Well, sir," said he, "I don't know whether we or the hand of death will be called on to quiet them"—he paused for an instant with uplifted hand; the roar and crash and wail of the city-wide riot surged into the gap of his silence—"but if it is we," he went on, "our little arrangements are made. My men know what to do, and my men are on the job," he concluded proudly.

The Sign at Six

Lyons nodded again.

"We have all done our best," said he. "Now, gentlemen, I do not see how we can possibly accomplish anything more by remaining here. My automobile is in concealment in the old stable in the rear of 127. My yacht is standing off the Battery awaiting signal to come in. We have," he glanced at his watch, "over an hour before the threatened catastrophe."

He looked up expectantly. The men all glanced uneasily at one another, except Simmons, who stared at his batteries stolidly.

"Come, gentlemen," urged Lyons, after a moment. "There is really not much time to lose, for you know the yacht must steam beyond the danger zone."

"Beat it," spoke up Simmons, at last. "There ain't any good of you here. If anything comes in, I can handle it. It's just a case of send out orders to your bulletin men."

"I think I'd better stay," observed Paige, the

225

The Sign at Six

stout young man, with an air of apology. "I know I'm not much use; but I've placed men, and they'll stick; and if this freeze-out proposition goes through—why, they're in it, and—"

"That's how I feel," broke in Perkins. "But you have done your full duty, Mr. Lyons, and you have no reason to stay. Let me get your car around to you—"

"Oh, I'm going to stay," said Lyons. "If you gentlemen feel it your duty, how much more is it mine! Professor Eldridge"—he bowed to the scientist—"you have done your best, which is more than any other mortal man could have done, I am sure; and you, sir—" he said to Hallowell.

Eldridge and Hallowell shook their heads.

"I have failed," said Eldridge.

"I am a reporter," said Hallowell.

"We are in the hands of God," announced Lyons with great solemnity, and folded his hands over his white waistcoat.

The Sign at Six

At that moment the door slowly swung open and Percy Darrow entered. He was smoking a cigarette, his hands were thrust deep in his trousers pockets; he was hatless, and his usually smooth hair was rumpled. A tiny wound showed just above the middle of his forehead, from which a thin stream of blood had run down to his eyebrows. He surveyed the room with a humorous twinkle shining behind his long lashes.

"Well, well, well, well!" he remarked in a cheerful tone of voice. "This is a nice, jolly, Quaker meeting! Why don't you get out and make a noise and celebrate, like your friends outside?"

"Thought you'd ducked," remarked Hallowell. The others said nothing, but looked a grave disapproval.

Darrow laughed.

"No, I had to come back to see how Eldridge is getting on." He cast a glance at the sci-

The Sign at Six

entist. "How goes it, old socks?" he inquired.

The man's manner, the tone of his voice, seemed as much out of place in this atmosphere of solemnity as a penny whistle in a death chamber. Darrow refused to notice the general attitude of disapproval, but planted himself in front of Eldridge.

"All in?" he challenged. "Or do you still cherish any delusions that you will get your man inside of"—he looked at his watch—"eleven minutes?"

A visible stir ran through the room at these words. "Eleven minutes!" murmured Lyons, and held his watch to his ear. "It has stopped," he said aloud. "It seems, gentlemen, that the only possible hope for us lies in the doubt as to whether or not this Unknown will carry out this threat."

"He's a first-rate hand to carry out threats," observed Darrow.

"We have done our best," said Lyons calmly.

The Sign at Six

"Let us compose ourselves to meet everything —or nothing—as the fates may have decided."

"That's all right," agreed Darrow, with unabated cheerfulness. "But Eldridge and I had a little agreement, or bet. He bragged he'd get this Monsieur X before I did. I'd like to know how he feels about his end of it. Give it up?"

Eldridge looked at him rebukingly.

"I have failed," he acknowledged formally, "from lack of time to carry out my investigation."

"From lack of brains," said Darrow brutally, "as I believe you once said in private conversation about my old master, Doctor, Schermerhorn. Those things are remembered. I am delighted to hand this back to you." He eyed Eldridge, the brilliant smile still curving his lips.

"Enough of this!" cried Lyons with authority. "This is unseemly in the face of eternity."

The Sign at Six

Darrow looked again at his watch.

"We have still six minutes, sir; and this is an affair of long standing, and on which I feel deeply. The score is settled," he said with entire respect. "I am now at your command. I had intended," he went on in a frivolous tone again, "to kick to you on my gas bill. It is too large. You, as responsible head, know it is. But somehow, you know, the presence here of you gentlemen has disarmed me. You don't need to be here; you all have the facilities to get away. Here you are! I guess you can charge a dollar and a quarter for gas if you want to." He looked from one to the other, while he carefully wiped back the blood that was flowing from the little wound in his forehead. "Eldridge acknowledges he has failed," he repeated.

"I fail to see how you have improved upon that failure," snapped Eldridge, stung.

"No?" queried Darrow. "I call Hallowell

The Sign at Six

to witness that the game has been fair. We had an even start; the data have been open to both." He raised his voice a little. "Jack!" he called.

Immediately through the open door from the hall outside came Jack Warford, leading by the arm a strange and nondescript figure. It was that of a small, bent, old-looking man, dressed in a faded suit of brown. His hair was thin, and long, and white; his face sharp and lean. His gaze was fixed straight before him, so that every one in the room at the same instant caught the glare of his eyes.

They were fixed, those eyes, like an owl's; or, better, a wildcat's, as though they never winked. From the pupils, which were very small, the little light-colored lines radiated across very large blue irises. There was something baleful and compelling in their glare, so that even Hallowell, cool customer as he was, forgot immediately all about the man's little-

The Sign at Six

ness and shabbiness and bent figure, and was conscious only of the cruel, clever, watchful, unrelenting, hostile spirit. As Jack dragged him forward, the others could see that one foot shambled along the floor.

"Gentlemen," observed Darrow in his most casual tones, "let me present Monsieur X!"

Every one exclaimed at once. Above the hubbub came Lyons' voice, clear and commanding.

"The proof!" he thundered. "This is too serious a matter for buffoonery. The proof!"

Percy Darrow raised his hand. Through he roar of the maddened city the bell of the Metropolitan tower was beginning its chimes. By the third stroke the uproar had died almost away. The people were standing still, awaiting what might come.

The sweet-toned chimes ceased. There succeeded the pause. Then the great bell began to boom.

The Sign at Six

One—two—three—four—five—six came its spaced and measured strokes. The last reverberations sank away. Nothing happened. Percy Darrow let his hand fall.

"The proof," he repeated, "is that you are still here."

From the night outside rose a wild shriek of rejoicing, stupendous, overwhelming, passionate. Paige sprang across the room. "Release!" he shouted fairly in Simmons' ear. The spark crashed. And at a dozen places simultaneously bulletins flashed; at a dozen other points placarded balloons arose, on which the search-lights played; so that the people, hesitating in their flight in thankfulness over finding themselves still alive, raised their eyes and read:

Monsieur X is captured. You are safe.

At that a tumult arose, a tumult of rejoicing. Darrow had sauntered to the window, and

The Sign at Six

was looking out. From the great height of the Atlas Building he could see abroad over much of the city. Here and there, like glowing planets, hung the balloons.

"Clever idea," he observed. "I'm glad you thought of it."

Hallowell was on his feet, his eyes shining.

"I've got the only paper on the job!" he fairly shouted. "Darrow, as you love me, give me the story. Where was he? Where did you get him?"

Darrow turned from the window, and sardonically surveyed Eldridge.

"He was in the office next door," said he, after a moment.

CHAPTER XXII

THE MAN NEXT DOOR

WHEN, three hours previous, Darrow had arisen with the remark before chronicled, Jack Warford had followed him in the expectation of a long expedition. To the young man's surprise it lasted just to the hall. There Darrow stopped before the blank door of an apparently unused office. Into the lock of this he cautiously fitted a key, manipulated it for a moment, and turned to Jack with an air of satisfaction.

"You have your gun with you?" he asked.

Jack patted his outside pocket.

"Very well, now listen here: I am going to leave the key in the lock. If you hear me

235

The Sign at Six

whistle sharply, get in as quickly as you know how, and get to shooting. Shoot to kill. If it happens to be dark and you can not make us out, shoot both. Take no chances. On your quickness and your accuracy may depend the lives of the whole city. Do you understand?"

"I understand," said Jack steadily. "Are you sure you can make yourself heard above all this row?"

Darrow nodded, and slipped inside the door.

He found the office chamber unlighted save by the subdued illumination that came in around the drawn shades of the window. Against the dimness he could just make out the gleaming of batteries in rows. An ordinary deal table supported a wireless sender. A figure stood before the darkened window, the figure of a little, old, bent man facing as though looking out. Through the closed casement the roar of the panic-stricken city sound-

The Sign at Six

ed like a flood. The old man was in the attitude of one looking out intently. Once he raised both arms, the fists clenched, high above his head.

Darrow stole forward as quietly as he could. When he was about half-way across the room the old man turned and saw him. For the briefest instant he stared at the intruder; then, with remarkable agility, cast himself toward the table on which stood the wireless sender. Darrow, too, sprang forward. They met across the table. Darrow clutched the old man's wrists.

Immediately began a desperate and silent trial of strength. The old man developed an unexpected power. The table lay between them, prohibiting a closer grip. Inch by inch, impelled by the man's iron will, his hand forced his way toward the sending key. Darrow put forth all his strength to prevent. There was no violent struggle, no noise; sim-

The Sign at Six

ply the pressure of opposing forces. Gradually the scientist's youth prevailed against the older man's desperation. The hand creeping toward the sender came to a stop. Then, all at once, the older man's resistance collapsed entirely. Darrow swept his arm back, stepped around the table, and drew his opponent, almost unresisting, back to the window.

"Jack!" he called.

At the sound of his voice the old man gathered his last vitality in a tremendous effort to jerk loose from his captor. Catching Darrow unawares, he almost succeeded in getting free. The flash was too brief. He managed only to rap the young man's head rather sharply against a shade-fitting of the window.

The outer door jerked open, and Jack Warford leaped into the room, revolver in hand. Darrow called an instant warning.

"All right!" he shouted. "Turn on the light, next you somewhere. Shut the door."

The Sign at Six

These orders were obeyed. The electric flared. By its light the office was seen to be quite empty save for a cabinet full of books and papers; rows and rows of battery jars; the receiving and sending apparatus of a wireless outfit; the deal table, and one wooden chair. Darrow looked around keenly.

"That's all right, Jack," said he. "Just get around here cautiously and raise the window shade. Look out you don't get near that table. That's it. Now just help me get this man a little away from the table! Good! Now, tie him up. No, bring over the chair. Tie him in that chair. Gently. That's all right. Whew!"

"You're hurt," said Jack.

Darrow touched his forehead.

"A bump," he said briefly. "Well, Jack, my son, we've done it!"

"You don't mean to say—" cried Jack.

Darrow nodded.

"Now, my friend," he addressed the hud-

239

The Sign at Six

dled figure in the chair, "the game is up. You are caught, and you must realize it." He surveyed the captive thoughtfully. "Tell me, who are you?" he added. "I should know you, for you are a great discoverer."

The old man stared straight at his interlocutor with his expressionless eyes, behind which no soul, no mind, no vitality even seemed to lie.

Darrow asked him several more questions, to which he received no replies. The man sat like a captured beast.

"I'm sorry," said Darrow to Jack. "I should like to have talked with him. Such a man is worth knowing; he has delved deep."

"He'll talk yet, when he gets over his grouch," Jack surmised.

But Darrow shook his head.

"The man is imbecile," he said. "He has been mentally unbalanced; and his disorder has grown on him lately. When I drove back his wrist just now the cord snapped in his brain."

The Sign at Six

Jack turned to stare at the captive.

"By Jove, I believe you're right!" said he at last.

Darrow was standing looking down on the deal table.

"Come here, Jack," said he, "I want you to look at the deadliest engine of destruction ever invented or wielded by mortal man. I suspect that if you were to reach out your hand and hold down the innocent-looking telegraph key there you would instantly destroy every living creature in this city."

Jack turned a little pale, and put both hands behind him.

Darrow laughed. "Feel tempted?" he inquired.

"Makes me a little dizzy, like being on a height," confessed Jack. "How's the trick turned?"

"I don't know," said Darrow. "I'm going to find out if I can."

The Sign at Six

Without attempting to touch anything, he proceeded to examine carefully every detail of the apparatus.

"The batteries are nothing extraordinary, except in strength," he told Jack, "and as near as I can make out the instrument is like any other. It must be some modification in the sending apparatus, some system of 'tuning', perhaps—it's only a surmise. We'll just disconnect the batteries," he concluded, "before we go to monkeying."

He proceeded carefully and methodically to carry out his expressed intention. When he had finished the task he heaved a deep sigh of relief.

"I'm glad you feel that way, too," said Jack. "I didn't know what might not happen."

"Me, either," confessed Darrow. "But now I think we're safe."

He proceeded on a methodical search through the intricacies of the apparatus. For

The Sign at Six

a time Jack followed him about, but after a while wearied of so profitless an occupation, and so took to smoking on the window-ledge. Darrow extended his investigations to the bookcase, and to a drawer in the deal table. For over two hours he sorted notes, compared, and ruminated, his brows knit in concentration. Jack did not try to interrupt him. At the end of the time indicated, the scientist looked up and made some trivial remark.

"Got it?" asked Jack.

"Yes," replied Darrow soberly. He reflected for several minutes longer; then moved to the window and looked out over the city. Absolutely motionless there he stood while the night fell, oblivious alike to the roar and crash of the increasing panic and to the silent figures in the darkened room behind him. At last he gave a sigh, walked quietly to the electric light, and turned it on.

"It's the biggest thing—and the simplest—

The Sign at Six

the world has ever known in physics, Jack,"
said he, "but it's got to go."

"What?" asked Jack, rousing from the
mood of waiting into which he had loyally
forced himself in spite of the turmoil outside.

"The man has perfected a combined system
of special tuning and definite electrical energy," said Darrow, "by which through an ordinary wireless sender he can send forth into
the ether what might be called deadening or
nullifying waves. You are no doubt familiar
with the common experiment by which two
sounds will produce a silence. This is just like
that. By means of this, within the radius of
his sending instrument and for a period of time
up to the capacity of his batteries, a man can
absolutely stop vibration of either heat, sound,
light, or electricity length. It is entirely a question of simple formulas. Here they are."

He held out four closely written pages
bound together with manuscript fasteners.

The Sign at Six

"No man has ever before attained this knowledge or this power," went on Darrow, after a moment; "and probably never again in the history of the race will exactly this combination of luck and special talent occur. These four pages are unique."

He laid them on the edge of the table, produced a cigarette, lighted it, picked up the four pages of formulas, and held the burning match to their edges. The flame caught, flared up the flimsy paper. Darrow dropped the burning corners as it scorched his fingers. It fell to the floor, flickered, and was gone.

Jack leaped forward with an exclamation of dismay. The old man bound to the chair did not wink, but stared straight in front of him, his eyes fixed like those of an owl or a wild-cat.

"For God's sake, Darrow!" cried Jack Warford. "Do you know what you have done?"

"Perfectly," replied Darrow calmly. "This

The Sign at Six

is probably the greatest achievement of the scientific intellect; but it must go. It would give to men an unchecked power that belongs only to the gods."

CHAPTER XXIII

HOW IT ALL WAS

FOR his share in the foregoing Percy Darrow was extensively blamed. It was universally conceded that his action in permitting Monsieur X to continue his activities up to the danger point was inexcusable. The public mind should have been reassured long before. Much terror and physical suffering might thus have been avoided—not to speak of financial loss. Scientific men, furthermore, went frantic over his unwarranted destruction of the formulas. Percy Darrow was variously described as a heartless monster and a scientific vandal. To these aspersions he paid no attention whatever.

The Sign at Six

Helen Warford, however, became vastly indignant and partisan, and in consequence Percy Darrow's course in the matter received from her its full credit for a genuine altruism. Hallowell, also, held persistently to this point, as far as his editors would permit him, until at last, the public mind somewhat calmed, attention was more focused on the means by which the man had reached his conclusions rather than on the use of them he had made.

The story was told three times by its chief actor: once to the newspapers, once to the capitalists from whom he demanded the promised reward, and once to the Warfords. This last account was the more detailed and interesting.

It was of a late afternoon again. The lamps were lighted, and tea was forward. Helen was manipulating the cups, Jack was standing ready to pass them, Mr. and Mrs. Warford sat in the background listening, and Darrow lounged gracefully in front of the fire.

248

The Sign at Six

"From the beginning!" Helen was commanding him, "and expect interruptions."

"Well," began Darrow, "it's a little difficult to get started. But let's begin with the phenomena themselves. I've told you before, how, when I was in jail, I worked out their nature and the fact that they must draw their power from some source that could be exhausted or emptied. You have read Eldridge's reasoning as to why he thought Monsieur X was at a distance and on a height. He took as the basis of his reasoning one fact in connection with the wireless messages we were receiving—that they were faint, and therefore presumably far distant or sent by a weak battery. He neglected, or passed over as an important item of tuning, the further fact that the instrument in the Atlas Building was the only instrument to receive Monsieur X's messages.

"Now, that fact might be explained either

The Sign at Six

on the very probable supposition that our receiving instrument happened in what we may call its undertones to be the only one tuned to the sending instrument of Monsieur X; or it might be because our instrument was nearer Monsieur X's instrument than any other. This was unlikely because of the quality of the sound—it sounded to the expert operator as though it came from a distance. Nevertheless, it was a possibility. Taken by itself, it was not nearly so good a possibility as the other. Therefore, Eldridge chose the other.

"There were a number of other strictly scientific considerations of equal importance. I do not hesitate to say that if I had been influenced only by the scientific considerations, I should have followed Eldridge's lead without the slightest hesitation. But as I told him at the time, a man must have imagination and human sympathy to get next to this sort of thing.

The Sign at Six

"Leaving all science aside, for the moment, what do we find in the messages to McCarthy? First, a command to leave within a specified and brief period; second, a threat in case of disobedience. That threat was always carried out."

Darrow turned to Mrs. Warford.

"With your permission, I should like to smoke," said he. "I can follow my thought better."

"By all means," accorded the lady.

Darrow lighted his cigarette, puffed a moment, and continued:

"For instance, at three o'clock he threatens to send a 'sign' unless McCarthy leaves town by six. McCarthy does not leave town. Promptly at six the 'sign' comes. What do you make of it?"

Nobody stirred.

"Why," resumed Darrow, "how, if Monsieur X was a hundred miles or so away, as El-

251

The Sign at Six

dridge figured, did he know that McCarthy had not obeyed him? We must suppose, from the probable fact of that knowledge, that either Monsieur X had an accomplice who was keeping him informed, or he must be near enough to get the information himself."

"There is a third possibility," broke in Jack. "Monsieur X might have sent along his 'sign' at six o'clock, anyhow, just for general results."

Darrow nodded his approval.

"Good boy, Jack," said he. "That is just the point I could not be sure about. But finally, at the time, you will remember, when I predicted McCarthy's disappearance, Monsieur X made a definite threat. He said," observed Darrow, consulting one of the bundle of papers he held in his hand:

" 'My patience is at an end. Your last warning will be sent you at nine-thirty this morning. If you do not sail on the *Celtic* at noon,

The Sign at Six

I shall strike,' and so forth. The *Celtic* sailed at noon, without McCarthy. At twelve thirty came the first message to the people calling on them to deliver up the 'traitor that is among you.' How did Monsieur X know that McCarthy had not sailed on the *Celtic?* The answer is now unavoidable: either an accomplice must have sent him word to that effect, or he must have determined the fact for himself.

"I eliminated the hypothesis of an accomplice on the arbitrary grounds of plain common sense. They don't grow two such crazy men at once; and one crazy man is naturally too suspicious to hire help. I took it for granted. Had to make a guess somewhere; but, contrary to our legal friends, I believe that enough coincidences indicate a certainty. But if Monsieur X himself saw the *Celtic* sail without McCarthy, and got back to his instrument within a half-hour, it was evident he could not

The Sign at Six

be quite so far away as Eldridge and the rest of them thought."

"One thing," spoke up Jack, "I often wondered what you whispered to Simmons to induce him to pass those messages over to you. Mind telling?"

"Not a bit. Simmons is an exceptional man. He has nerve and intelligence. I just pointed out to him the possibility that Monsieur X might have control over heat vibrations. He saw the public danger at once, and realized that McCarthy's private rights in those messages had suddenly become very small."

Jack nodded. "Go ahead," said he.

"I had already," proceeded Darrow, "found out where the next wireless station is located. Monsieur X must be nearer the Atlas station than to this other. It was, therefore, easy to draw a comparatively small circle within which he must be located."

"So far, so good," said Helen. "How did

The Sign at Six

you finally come to the conclusion that Monsieur X was in the next office?"

"Do you remember," Darrow asked Jack, "how the curtain of darkness hung about ten or twelve feet inside the corridor of the Atlas Building?"

"Sure," replied Jack.

"And do you remember that while the rest of you, including Eldridge, were occupied rather childishly with the spectacular side of it, I had disappeared inside the blackness?"

"Certainly."

"Well, in that time I determined the exact extent of the phenomena. I found that it extended in a rough circle. And when I went outside and looked up—something every one else was apparently too busy to do—I saw that this phenomenon of darkness also extended above the building, out into open space. At the moment I noted the fact merely, and tried to fix in my own mind approximately the di-

The Sign at Six

mensions. Then here is another point: when the city-wide phenomena took place, I again determined their extent. To do so I did not have to leave my chair. The papers did it for me. They took pains to establish the farthest points to which these modern plagues of Manhattan reached."

Darrow selected several clippings from his bundle of papers.

"Here are reports indicating Highbridge, Corona, Flatbush, Morrisania, Fort Lee, Bay Ridge as the farthest points at which the phenomena were manifested. It occurred to nobody to connect these points with a pencil line. If that line is made curved, instead of straight, it will be found to constitute a complete circle *whose center is the Atlas Building!"*

The audience broke into exclamations.

"Going back to my former impressions, I remembered that the pall of blackness extended this far and that far in the various directions,

The Sign at Six

so that it required not much imagination to
visualize it as a sphere of darkness. And
strangely enough the center of that sphere
seemed to be located somewhere near the floor
on which were installed the United Wireless
instruments. It at once became probable that
what we may call the nullifying impulses radiated in all directions through the ether from
their sending instrument.

"Next I called upon the janitor of the Atlas
Building, representing myself as looking for a
suitable office from which to conduct my investigations. In this manner I gained admis-
sion to all unrented offices. All were empty.
I then asked after the one next door, but was
told it was rented as a storeroom by an ec-
centric gentleman now away on his travels.
That was enough. I now knew that we had
to do with a man next door, and not miles
distant, as purely scientific reasoning would
seem to prove."

The Sign at Six

"But Professor Eldridge's experiments—" began Jack.

"I am coming to that," interrupted Darrow. "When Eldridge began to call up Monsieur X, that gentleman answered without a thought of suspicion; nor was he even aware of the very ingenious successive weakenings of the current. In fact, as merely the thickness of a roof separated his receiving instrument from the wires from which the messages were sent, it is probable that Eldridge might have weakened his current down practically to nihil, and still Monsieur X would have continued to get his message."

"Wouldn't he have noticed the sending getting weaker?" asked Jack shrewdly.

"Not until the very last. Our sending must have made a tremendous crash, anyway, and he probably read it by sound through the wall."

"But at about the fifty-mile limit of sending we lost him," objected Jack.

258

The Sign at Six

"You mean at about two o'clock in the morning," amended Darrow.

"Eh? Yes, it was about two. But how did he get on to what Eldridge was doing?"

"He read it in the paper," replied Darrow. "At twelve the reporters left. At a little before two our enterprising friend, the *Despatch*, issued an extra in its usual praiseworthy effort to enlighten the late Broadway jag. Monsieur X read it, and knew exactly what was up."

"How do you know?"

"Because I read the extra myself."

"But even then?"

"Then he began to pay more attention. It was easy enough to fake when he knew what was doing. For all I know, he could hear Eldridge giving his directions."

The company present ruminated over the disclosures thus far made.

"About the City Hall affair?" asked Helen finally.

The Sign at Six

"I used to sit where I could command the hall," said Darrow, "and, therefore, I was aware that Monsieur X never left his room. To make the matter certain, I powdered the sill of the door with talcum, which I renewed every day after the cleaners. You remember we got to talking very earnestly in the hall, so earnestly that I, for one, forgot to watch. When I realized my remissness, I saw that the powder on the sill had been disturbed, that Monsieur X had gone out.

"My first thought then was to warn the people. To that end I was on my way to the *Despatch* office when sheer chance switched me into the City Hall tragedy. I possessed myself of the apparatus—"

"That was the square black bag!" cried Jack.

"Of course—and hustled back to the Atlas Building. You can bet I was relieved when I found that Monsieur X had returned to his lair."

The Sign at Six

"Talcum disturbed again?" asked Jack.

"Precisely."

"And the black bag?"

"Contained merely a model wireless apparatus with a clockwork arrangement set to close the circuit at a certain time. That is why Monsieur X was not involved in his own catastrophe."

"I see!"

"Then all I had to do was to sit still and wait for him to become dangerous."

"How did you dare to take such chances?" cried Helen.

"I took no chances," answered Darrow. "Don't you see? If he were to attempt to destroy the city, he must either involve himself in the destruction, or he must set another bit of clockwork. If he had left his office again I should have seized him, broken into the office, and smashed the apparatus."

"But he was crazy," spoke up Mrs. Warford. "How could you rely on his not involving himself in the general destruction?"

"Yes, why did you act when you did?" seconded Helen.

"As long as he held to his notion of getting hold of McCarthy," explained Darrow, "he had a definite object in life, his madness had a definite outlet—he was harmless. But the last message showed that his disease had progressed to the point where McCarthy was forgotten. His mind had risen to a genuine frenzy. He talked of general punishments, great things. At last he was in the state of mind of the religious fanatic who lacerates his flesh and does not feel the wound. When he forgot McCarthy, I knew it was time to act. Long since I had provided myself with the requisite key. You know the rest."

CHAPTER XXIV

WHAT HAPPENED AFTERWARD

THERE remains only to tell what became
of the various characters of the tale.

McCarthy, on whom the action started, returned, but never regained his political hold.
Darrow always maintained that this was only
the most obvious result of his policy of delay-
ing the dénouement. People had been forced
to think seriously of such matters; and, when
aroused, the public conscience is right.

Darrow demanded, and received, the large
money reward for his services in the matter.
Pocketing whatever blame the public and his
fellow scientists saw fit to hand out to him,
he and Jack Warford disappeared in command

The Sign at Six

of a small schooner. The purpose of the expedition was kept secret; its direction was known only to those most intimately concerned. If it ever returns, we may know more of it.

Eldridge went on being a scientist, exactly as before.

Simmons received a gold medal, a large cash sum, any amount of newspaper space, and an excellent opportunity to go on a vaudeville circuit.

Hallowell had his salary raised; and received in addition that rather vague brevet title of "star reporter".

Helen Warford is still attractive and unmarried. Whether the latter condition is only pending the return of the expedition is not known.

As for the city, it has gone back to its everyday life, and the riffles on the surface have smoothed themselves away. In outside ap-

The Sign at Six

pearances everything is as before. Yet for the present generation, at least, the persistence of the old independent self-reliance of the people is assured. They have been tested, and they have been made to think of elemental things seriously. For some time to come the slow process of standardization has been arrested.

THE END

www.ingramcontent.com/pod-product-compliance
Lightning Source LLC
Chambersburg PA
CBHW020649030726
47498CB00002B/436